THE ROAD HOME

By Jeanna Knoll

May you always find your road home.

Love,
Jeanna

Jeanna Knoll

DEDICATION

This book is dedicated with love to my dad, Milton "Mike" Knoll, Jr. (1952 – 2010), and to all the family and friends I grew up with and seemingly left behind on my life's journey. I did not leave you or forget you for I carry pieces of each and every one of you in my heart, wherever I go. You all helped to shape my character and my life. Each of you is an integral piece of my road home.

Dad assembling Jeanna's birthday present, May 28, 1975

AUTHOR'S NOTE

This is a complete work of fiction. Some historical events have been mentioned throughout the story in order to better evoke the time period, but other than that, any resemblance characters, places, and events in the story bear to actual people, places, and events is purely coincidental or anecdotal and due mainly to the fact that I believe the best stories are born in the place where memories and imagination collide.

That being said, I wrote this particular story for several reasons. The impetus was an essay I wrote for my hometown of Conde, South Dakota's quasquicentennial, a walk through the town on the way to school as I remembered it when I was a little girl. The beginning of the essay provided an explanation:

Have you ever watched those shows on the History channel where archeologists, historians, and sociologists try to recreate the scene and tell a story of the day to day lives of the people in long lost civilizations simply by sifting through centuries old rubble of buildings that once stood, tiny shards of pottery, and broken bits of refuse? Those shows always amaze me. What fabulous imaginations those people have. While watching them spin their fantastic tales, I imagine what the real people of those long lost civilizations might think of those stories. My guess would be that the experts are way, way off and it was nothing like that at all.

With the closing of the school, the demolition of the old buildings on Main Street, and the passing of so many treasured "grownups" from my childhood, I've started to feel as if all trace of my life is disappearing behind me and soon no one will ever know I existed. There will not be any rubble for the archeologists, historians, and sociologists of the future to sift through to recreate my story.

The tiny little world in which I existed as a child is already vastly different than it was then and soon will be lost completely, never to be recovered. There should be something I can do to stop that from happening, some little way that I can at least preserve a piece of my soon to be lost civilization. I guess I will just have to tell my own story before I leave.

I had so much fun writing the essay and so many people commented on how well what I remembered matched their memories and made them remember other things they hadn't thought of in years. I loved that it had that effect on people.

My dad told me if I opened a book, I could explore every place ever, all of this world and all of the make-believe worlds ever dreamed up, this time, past time, and future time, every place ever...and still be home in time for supper. I loved that idea. I read voraciously as a kid. I couldn't wait to leave the sleepy, tiny, rural community in northeastern South Dakota where I was born and raised and actually go places. I dreamed of traveling the world, living exciting adventures, and being a writer, taking other people with me on my travels through the books I would write. Somehow everyday life and my own defeatist thoughts obscured my dream of becoming a writer.

It's been decades now since I was that idealistic little girl, sitting in a haystack, reading, and dreaming of the big, wide world beyond the prairie. I did not travel the world, but I did leave that little town and live a few adventures. I have been to quite a few places in the intervening years, but now that I am so much older in so many ways, I have realized that the only place I really want to go is the place I couldn't wait to leave and now it's not there anymore, at least not the way I remember it.

One of my all time favorite novels is *To Kill a Mockingbird*. I love that book not because of its deep meaning or social commentary, but because when I read it, I felt like I was Scout, growing up in a small town in the South in the 1930's. Harper Lee described the time and place where she grew up so well that she made you feel like you were there too. I have read a lot of books in my time, but I have never read a book about the time and place where I grew up.

According to Merriam-Webster Dictionary, the definition of the word *essence* is: *the basic nature of a thing; the quality or qualities that make a thing what it is; a substance that contains in very strong form, the special qualities of the thing from which it comes or is taken.* I will repeat, this story is fictional, but my hope is that it will evoke the essence of the special people, time, and place from which I come.

*"It was 1970-somethin',
in the world that I grew up in...."*

-from the song, *19 Somethin'*,
written by David Lee and Chris Dubois
and performed and recorded by Mark Wills

one

"Oh, Virgil, look," I exclaimed, "sundogs!"

"What?"

I clutched my best friend Virgil's mitten clad hand in my own and pointed to the sky. "Look, sundogs! It's going to snow today."

"How do you know?"

I leaned my head close to his and pointed to the sky again. "See how it looks like there are four suns, a big one and then three smaller ones, with a line of light going through the middle of them all, connecting them together?"

"Yeah, but how do you know it's gonna snow?"

"Great Grandma Sophie told me they were called sundogs because they look like sled dogs running through the sky, the line of light connecting them their traces as they pull a big sled full of snow. When you catch sight of them, their sled tips over and snow pours out."

"Huh. I guess they could kinda look like sled dogs if you squint and use your imagination."

"I think the scientific explanation is something about sunlight reflecting off of ice crystals in the clouds, but I would much rather imagine giant sled dogs racing across the sky spilling snow from their sled, wouldn't you?"

"Yeah, giant sled dogs are much cooler."

It did start snowing that afternoon, not long before school let out. The snow was falling in big, fluffy, three-dimensional flakes, my favorite kind, not too wet and not too dry.

Just the morning before over breakfast, Grandpa Oscar and I had discussed the merits of different types of snowflakes. I loved having breakfast with Grandpa Oscar and Grandma Mae. Grandma made me hot, sugary Cream of Wheat and toast with honey and she carefully cut and sectioned a grapefruit for Grandpa, placing it in his special yellow bowl. We sat on the green vinyl bench seats of the breakfast nook and enjoyed our meal.

"Grandpa, did you know that there are at least five different kinds of snowflakes? I'm pretty sure there are way more than five, I just haven't written any others down in my notebook yet."

"Five kinds, huh? Can't say as I've noticed, Jennie Girl. Snow is snow."

"Oh no, Grandpa, let me tell ya. Some snowflakes are too wet and fall like big globs of slush. That kind is good for making igloos or snow forts because it packs good and it gets hard and iced over, but bad for snowballs because it doesn't explode, so it feels like getting hit by a super fast baseball pitch. Some snowflakes are flat crystals that look just like the paper snowflakes we make in school, they're really pretty to look at when they stick to the window glass, and they sparkle like diamonds when the sun hits them, but they aren't good for much besides looking pretty. The really good kind of snowflakes are big and fluffy, so they don't hurt when they hit your skin, and they're beautiful to look at because they're like four or five flat snowflakes connected by their middles to make a spinning, sparkling globe like a Christmas tree ornament. They're wet enough to pack good, but not wet enough to ice over, so they make exploding snowballs and easy to shape snowmen. They're just wet enough to make the runners of a sled glide nice, but fluffy and dry enough to be soft when you crash. That kind is the perfect snowflake. There are lots of kinds of snowflakes and I haven't even cataloged them all yet. Cataloging things is what scientists do, by the way. I learned that in school a few weeks back. I like practicing being a scientist, just in case I decide to become one someday."

"Well, that was very informative." Grandpa shook his head and chuckled. "You do like to ruminate, child."

"What's ruminate?"

"It means study things or think on them for a long time…chew them over and over slowly like a cow chews a cud."

"Huh. I like that word. I'm going to add it to my 'Words I Like' list. We just learned in school last week why cows chew cuds all day. Do you know why?"

"Well, I'd be interested to hear your version, Little Bird." Grandpa Oscar called me Little Bird sometimes because he said I chirped and chirped nonstop, just like a hungry little bird.

"A cud is the wad of regurgitated guck a cow chews in the back of her mouth all day long. I like that word, regurgitated. It's one of those sound words, you know, it kind of sounds like what it means. ReGURGitate. The gurg part sounds like the noise you make when you're gagging or throwing up. I like when words do that."

"Okay, we're trying to eat breakfast here, Girly. Move on."

"Right. So, things like grass, hay, and silage, things cows eat for food, are really hard to digest. It takes a long time to do and four different stomachs to do it with. Well, only one of the stomachs is an actual stomach, but all four of what most people call stomachs are organs that perform digestive functions. Pretty much the way it works is that the cow chews up the grass or silage a little bit, sends it to stomach one where it swishes around a little and picks up some things called digestive enzymes, then she yaks it up and chews it again for awhile, sends it to stomach two where it picks up more goo, yaks it up and chews it again, and she keeps doing that until it gets through all the stomachs and comes out the other end. Cool, huh? I mean, in a really disgusting sort of way."

"Mmm. Cool."

Grandpa and I chewed for a few seconds, but it was hard for me to both sit still and be quiet at the same time.

"I got 100% on my spelling test yesterday."

"That's my girl."

"Grandma said we could make molasses cookies after school this afternoon."

"Sounds good."

"Did you know that Arabian horses have twenty three vertebrae and all the other kinds of horses have twenty four vertebrae?"

"I did not know that. Why would you know that?"

"Because I just started reading through Grandma's World Book Encyclopedias and Arabian is near the beginning."

"You're planning to read all of them?"

"Yep. I want to learn everything in them and then I figure I'll know about the whole world. I'll know lots of little known facts to help me solve mysteries like Encyclopedia Brown. People will call me Encyclopedia Ericson. That sounds pretty good, huh?"

"Hmm."

"You'll be home weekend after next, right? Because the children's choir is singing in church that Sunday so you'll come with Grandma, right?"

Grandpa shook his head again and said, "Following your conversations is like following a pinball being played by a highest score contender."

I scowled at him, shrugged, and continued on until Grandma Mae said I needed to shake a leg or I'd be late for school.

The snowflakes falling in northeastern South Dakota on the afternoon of Friday, January 10, 1975, were the perfect kind. The attribute I mentioned to Grandpa, that they're just wet enough to make the runners of a sled glide nice, but fluffy and dry enough to be soft when you crash, was what I was thinking about in particular on that day. I had gotten a brand new Flexible Flyer sled for Christmas and it was beautiful. It had a body of smooth, shiny, varnished wood with a very majestic and powerful looking insignia of an eagle clutching arrows in his talons in the middle. The runners and metal frame were bright red and a soft yellow rope controlled the steering bar on the front. There hadn't been a good snow since just before Christmas though, so I hadn't had a chance to really test it out. Dad had pulled me around the yard a few times, but I had yet to take a hill and during the perfect sledding snowfall seemed a fine opportunity to do so.

It wasn't too cold for January and the snow was falling fast and thick as Virgil and I bundled up for our walk home from school. Virgil and I lived across the street from each other at the opposite end of town from the school.

"Hey, Virgil, you wanna go sledding when we get home?"

"Can't."

"How come?"

"Mom said I have to come straight home today. She's timing me."

"Why?"

"I have to clean my room."

"This afternoon?"

"Yep."

"Why do you have to do it this afternoon?"

"Mom said if I don't do it right after school today, I can't have a birthday party on Monday."

"Well, that's no fun."

"Yeah, Mom's like that sometimes…especially when it gets hard to open my bedroom door."

After only walking a block or so, our neighbor, Mr. Olesen, saw us and stopped to pick us up and give us a ride home. Mr. Olesen was a fairly dependable ride home given that coming through town at that time of the day was part of his normal routine and he was happy to do so, if only to extol and demonstrate the virtues of his 1972 Ford Ranchero. Mr. Olesen's prized Ranchero was the Squire model with simulated wood-grain paneling along the flanks and a very complementary body color of pumpkin orange.

"Let me just toss your bags in the cargo bed, kids," Mr. Olesen said.

"You can do that because it's not just a car...," Virgil piped.

"...and not just a truck," I added.

"...but rather, a sporty and versatile coupe utility vehicle," Virgil continued.

"...which was adapted from a two door station wagon platform," I interjected.

"...and integrated the cab and cargo bed into the body," Virgil concluded.

Mr. Olesen scowled at us as we collapsed into giggles while piling into the cab.

I leaned over, kissed Mr. Olesen on the cheek, and gave him a crooked grin as I said, "We're sorry, Mr. Olesen. We were just teasing. We love your car, we like it when you tell us about it, and we're thankful when you give us a ride." He blushed and grumbled a little under his breath, but he let it go.

I was very happy to see Mr. Olesen that day as that meant I would get home at least half an hour earlier, giving me just a little bit more daylight in which to play in the perfect snow. He parked in his own driveway and Virgil and I thanked him for the ride, jumped out, and walked the half a block to our houses. The snow was falling steady, but there wasn't much wind yet.

"I'm still going to take the sled out, I think. This is the perfect snow for it. I don't want to miss my chance. Can you clean your room fast and meet me on the hill beside the Nagle farm?"

"I dunno. It's not looking good. I think it's gonna take me awhile."

"Well, okay," I sighed, "You don't want to not get a birthday party and the snow will still be here tomorrow."

"Right." Virgil turned left to head to his house and I turned right to head to mine.

As I neared the door, I turned to wave at Virgil and yelled, "Later, Alligator."

Virgil turned at his door and responded with, "After while, Crocodile."

Entering the back door, I hollered, "Hi, Mom! I'm home," shoved off my boots and tromped up the stairs to get my special sledding mittens with the leather patches on the palms and fingers that made my hands look like bear paws and served to further protect them from rope burn when steering the sled. I thought I hollered to Mom again before I went back out, but maybe not. She was used to me slamming in and out of the door at least a couple of times before I got all my stuff in the house, but I was focused and on a mission that day and only made one trip.

Our houses were the last ones on that edge of town. When the town was first laid out in the 1880s, our house was homestead acreage just outside the town proper. As a result, we had a huge yard that included a field Dad planted just like all his other fields out in the country and an old barn next to the house, but Dad didn't use it for anything. Dad was a farmer, but he did most of his farming with Papa out at Papa and Grandma Cori's house, which was a real, working farm with hundreds of acres about three miles outside of town. The road that bordered our yard and Virgil's yard to the east was the official city limit in 1975. The Nagle family owned all the land on the east side of the city limit road and had had an operating farm there with the usual fields, pastures, and outbuildings. The good sized hill near the Nagle farmhouse was the one I had deemed ideal for the Flexible Flyer's maiden, downhill voyage.

The snow was falling heavily now and it was getting hard to see. I was all bundled up, looking like the Michelin Man in my snow boots, snow pants, parka, scarf, stocking cap, and sledding mittens, so trudging across our city block long yard, across the street, and up the hill, pulling my sled behind me, took a lot more time and effort than I was anticipating. By the time I got to the top of the hill, it had grown much colder and the wind had picked up considerably. The snow looked like it was falling sideways instead of down and I couldn't see the bottom of the hill. I knew there was a big boulder somewhere at the base of the hill near the driveway and my plan was to sled to the right of said boulder, but it was a little slippery getting up the hill and I had to zigzag back and forth to get to the top, so I wasn't real sure anymore how far I was from the boulder. Trying to see to the bottom of the hill and not being able to make it out was the last thing I remembered.

two

One glowing, green eye floated near my face through the blowing snow. The thoughts in my head spun, tumbled, and fell like a Tilt-a-Whirl as I tried to figure out where I was, why there was only one eye, and why I and the eye seemed like disembodied objects bobbing in a cold white sea. Just as I was about to grab hold of a clear thought, a lightning strike of pain flashed through my head and the howling, white sea turned black and silent.

I awoke to the sound of the wind rattling my bedroom window. My head was nestled against Mom's chest, her slender hand cupping my cheek as she lay sleeping by my side atop the covers. I could feel a drop of water sliding from the wet washcloth on my forehead down my temple towards my ear. I can't stand to have just one drop of water anywhere on my skin. I am good with being immersed in water or even having one whole section of my body wet, like a hand or an arm or a leg, or lots of drops of water everywhere like playing in the rain or taking a shower, but I can't stand just one drop of wet. I feel one drop of wet on my skin way too much. As the air hits the wet little spot of skin, it tickles and makes me shiver way down deep inside, almost painfully, like the way it makes you shiver when you hear fingernails scrape against a chalkboard. You just feel compelled to make that kind of shiver stop and the only way to stop the one-drop-of-wet-shiver is to rub the wet spot dry. I couldn't. One hand was trapped under the covers next to Mom's body and though I felt the other hand clutching Bunny's arm, in my sleep induced fog, I couldn't figure out how to free it. I started to whimper in frustration, chanting commands in my head, "Must rub the wet spot dry. Stop the shiver. Hand, free the hand." My body was not cooperating. Nothing worked right.

Mom must have heard me then. She popped straight up, eyes wide and startled, swaying back and forth for a few seconds like my old Jack in the Box after you turned the crank through all but the last few notes of the *Pop Goes the Weasel* tune. Suddenly, she remembered what was happening and turned to bend over me, exclaiming, "Oh, thank goodness, you're awake!"

I was glad to have made her so happy simply by opening my eyes, but now she was leaning over me with one hand on either side of my body, trapping both of my hands beneath the covers. I licked my dry lips and croaked, "The drip."

"What, Baby?" She leaned close, "What's wrong? Are you okay? What hurts?"

I tried again. "Stop the drip," I whispered.

"Ripped? What's ripped? Nothing's ripped, Sweetheart."

Okay, now the drop of water was slithering into my outer ear, slipping and sliding over the super sensitive bumps and whorls on its way into my inner ear canal, making me shiver ever more deeply while envisioning an imagined scene from *Star Trek* as an alien life force slid into my brain to take over my body. I started to panic, weakly thrashing about, attempting to dislodge Mom and free my hands to stop the drip. Mom leapt off the bed to better survey the situation and position herself for restraining me if need be. As she moved, so did the restriction on the blankets and the hand I was struggling to free was unexpectedly released, flying into the air so that Bunny's plastic face smacked me in the head…squarely on top of the newly acquired, blue-green ringed goose egg on my forehead. The sudden pain left me gasping for air like a fish out of water, the drip forgotten.

"Settle down, Jennie. Don't touch it." Mom moved the wet washcloth from my pillow where it had slid during my struggle and started fussing with the blankets, straightening them out and refolding the top of the sheet neatly over the edge of the comforter. "Take a deep breath, slowly now, and let it out. There you go. Is that better?" She reached over to the bedside table for a glass of water and helped me sit up enough to take a few sips. Ah. That was better.

"Look at my finger. Now follow it. Follow my finger with your eye. Now this one," she waved a flashlight around my face then clicked it off. Having determined my death was not imminent, she turned to me with her arms crossed in her classic "you are in deep trouble" stance. "Jennie Marie Ericson, would you like to tell me just what were you doing outside in a blizzard? I thought you were up here in your room. You can't just wander off like that in the middle of winter without a word to anyone. What if you had gotten lost in the snow? You could have frozen to death. We looked everywhere for you. Your dad had to leave Papa to finish getting the barn ready for the cattle to take shelter so he could come help me look for you. Finally, I came back in the house to start calling your friends when I heard a banging noise and found you in the mudroom curled up asleep on a pile of Dad's coveralls. How did you get there?"

"Uh, I don't know."

"You don't know? How could you not know?"

"Uh, I don't think I remember. My head hurts. I don't feel so good."

"Well, get some rest then, I guess. You probably have a concussion from that bump on your head. I'm going to wake you up every couple of hours to check on you. We'll talk about this again later after Dad gets back from checking on the great grandparents. No one should be out in this weather and he wants to be sure they're all buttoned up."

I squeezed Bunny and tried to remember what had happened, but I just wasn't sure. I tried talking it out with Bunny. She was an excellent listener. Bunny wasn't really a bunny. She wasn't even really a fake bunny. She would have been a little creepy looking if I hadn't already loved her so much before I was old enough to recognize the creepy factor. Grandma Mae gave her to me for Easter when I was only two. I think she was supposed to be a baby dressed in a pink bunny costume, but all I noticed was the long ears and thought she was an actual bunny without realizing that an actual bunny with a human face and hands would be weird. Except for her plastic face and hands, Bunny was soft and snuggly, always offering just the right amount of comfort. She had pale blue silk in the inside of her long ears. The smooth, cool silk rubbing against my cheek was always soothing when I had had an upset or couldn't sleep. Bunny was starting to look just a little worse for wear. A bratty little kid Mom used to babysit bit off one of her plastic hands and Mom had to just sew up her wrist like her hand had been amputated. Her pink belly was getting a little threadbare, having been snuggled and loved too well over the years. Bunny was always there for me though, always providing comfort, understanding, and a listening ear...a long pink and blue one.

Bunny and I tried to figure out what had happened, but I was just too sleepy and my head was aching too much to concentrate. I drifted off into a restless sleep.

Dad was sitting on the side of my bed when I awoke next. "It appears you had quite a day, huh, First Born?" I heard him say as I opened my eyes. Dad started calling me First Born after my little sister Julie was born. I had lots of grandparents and aunts and uncles and I was the star attraction at our house until Julie showed up. All of a sudden, Julie got all my stuff, my old crib, my blankets, my clothes, my toys, and everybody was coming to our house to see the precious baby and not me. It didn't seem like anybody loved me anymore, they just wanted to "ooh" and "ahh" at baby Julie. I didn't get the appeal. It looked to me like all she did was sit there and drool. Dad caught me pouting one day when Julie, The Drooling Wonder, was holding court and figured out I wasn't happy with the new order of things. Dad sat me on his lap so we could have a serious talk. Serious talks were always better held on Dad's lap. Things always made more sense somehow if I could lay my head on his shoulder while he explained. Dad explained that he loved both his girls a whole big bunch, but that I was always going to have something extra special that Julie could never have. I couldn't think what that would be. Julie was getting all my stuff and all the attention, so what was left that was extra special? Dad went on to say that I would always be extra special because I would always be his first born child and no one on earth could ever be that but me. From then on, Dad always called me First Born when he thought I needed a little special attention.

"I guess I did."

"What were you doing out in the snow like that and how'd you get home? Your mom was worried. It's pretty dangerous to be out in the snow alone, you know."

"I'm not too sure what happened. It's kind of hard to see in my head and I'm not feeling that great."

"Well, now that you're safe in your bed, I guess it won't hurt anything for you to think on it a little and tell us about it in the morning. Let's get you tucked in good." Dad moved the covers up under my chin so I was all covered up. "Have you got room for your radiator?"

"Yep." I always slept completely covered up, all the way up to my neck, but always with one foot sticking out in the open air. It didn't matter how cold it was or how many blankets I had to snuggle under to keep the rest of my body warm, one foot still had to able to get out from under the blankets for me to be able to sleep. In the summer, when it was hot as blue blazes, I still had to be completely covered from head to toe, even if it was with just a sheet, but if that one foot could touch the air, I was comfortable. Mom and

Dad said I had always been that way. At just a few days old, if they swaddled me up like I was in a little blanket cocoon, I would scream my head off. After hours and hours of rocking and singing to no avail, they finally noticed that as soon as one foot got uncovered during the struggle, I would shut up and go to sleep. Dad told me my foot must regulate my body temperature in much the same way a radiator regulates engine temperature. Radiators need water to work and my foot needed air.

Long after Dad kissed me good night, I lay awake thinking and listening to the howling wind.

Weather on the Great Plains is like a living, breathing being, not just a description of atmospheric conditions. Our entire lives revolved around the weather. Every conversation I ever heard adults have both started and ended with some reference to or discussion of the weather, what it was doing now, what it was going to do later, or what it had done in either the recent or distant past. The weather was always referred to as a person-like entity unto itself, either It or The Weather. "It looks like rain." "The Weather is ugly today." "It hasn't come a storm like this since the summer of 1952." "What's The Weather look like to you?" "It might decide to warm up tomorrow." The Weather was a living thing to us, a mighty and powerful thing that controlled our very existence. The Weather was capable of either sustaining our lives or utterly destroying our lives, seemingly on a whim. It was able to bring us great riches or leave us penniless. It was even able to kill us outright in an instant. The Weather was moody and constantly changing. It didn't seem as if God controlled The Weather, or if He did, He either often didn't like us very much or felt we needed a great deal of testing.

Blizzards and tornadoes were The Weather in its meanest, most monster-like forms. Blizzards were the winter monsters. You could feel the winter monster's anger and cruelty in the howling winds blowing the biting ice and snow across the plains like the great beast was stomping across the land, swiping huge arms to and fro, freezing and killing every unprotected thing in its path. Tornadoes were the spring and summer monsters. They too were angry and cruel and stomped across the land, but they would crush things in their path or pick them up and hurl them through the air to smash them against the ground.

The Weather wasn't always cruel. It could bring warm sunshine or gentle rain, but living on the Great Plains, you always knew it could turn on you in the blink of an eye.

I stayed in bed late the following morning. Mom made me French toast for breakfast and let me eat it on the livingroom floor while I watched cartoons.

Mom and Julie and I stayed snuggled up in the house all day, but poor Dad had to get out to the farm to feed the cattle. It took an hour to drive the three miles through the blowing and drifting snow. Feeding the cattle took most of the day as he was only able to work for about fifteen minutes before being forced to go inside to thaw the ice from his eyelashes so he could see. During the night, the temperature had plummeted to nearly seventy degrees below zero. Temperatures that low make it hard to even breathe. It actually hurts to breathe quickly and deeply without breathing through a scarf or face mask to warm the air. Unfiltered, the air temperature is so cold it freezes the moisture in your lungs and bronchial tubes. You can throw a cup of boiling water in the air and it will turn to snow and blow away before it hits the ground. Dad wore a stocking cap, face mask, and scarf, but the steam from his breath would ice up on its way past his eyes and little icicles would cling to his eyelashes, the ice building up with each puff of breath, until the icicles got too thick to brush away and he couldn't see or it would freeze his eyes closed. He would have to go inside and drink another cup of coffee until his eyelashes thawed and he could go back out and try again.

The blizzard continued unabated throughout the day and night, so Dad stayed overnight at the farm. On Sunday, the snow and wind began to ease.

I watched the news with Dad and saw the reports of the damage done and the people and livestock killed. The blizzard conditions were even worse in eastern Minnesota where snow drifts of up to twenty feet paralyzed activity. Thousands of people were stranded either when they hit snow drifts on the road too thick to punch through or when their engines seized up and stopped after the cold turned the oil to sludge. One hundred sixty eight people were trapped overnight on a train in Wilmar, Minnesota. People, livestock, and property were lost throughout Minnesota and the Dakotas and some areas took more than ten days to clear. The blizzard losses, in addition to the Minnesota Vikings' Super Bowl loss to the Pittsburgh Steelers in New Orleans that Sunday, led many to refer to the blizzard famously as The Super Bowl Blizzard.

three

Monday dawned bright and clear. The landscape on the prairie was beautiful after a blizzard passed through. The bright sunlight combined with the cold, crisp temperature made everything look sharper and clearer, the blue of the sky and the white of the snow so intense they were almost blinding and made you blink for several seconds until your eyes adjusted.

The bad weather had passed, but school was still canceled as everyone needed to dig out before they could go anywhere. Sunday afternoon, Dad had driven the loader tractor home from the farm so that he'd have it at the house to clear the roads. Dad cleared our driveway, the Sinclair's, the next couple of neighbors', and the road in between our houses, pushing all of the snow into one big pile in our yard, then jumped off the tractor and hollered for me and Virgil. It was time to take a break and play a little King of the Mountain. Virgil and I had played this with Dad before and knew we had to team up in order to beat him before we could turn on each other.

"Rawr! Who's the King of Mountain?" Dad roared as he started stomping up the snow pile with his arms spread wide, acting like the Abominable Snowman from *Rudolph the Red Nosed Reindeer.*

Virgil and I pelted him with snowballs that he batted away with his big, gloved hands as he continued on. After a quick conference, we decided to split up. We went wide like we were planning to outflank him then looked at each other, and with a signal, both raced in and up the pile, leaping at the same time to throw our arms around Dad's legs and drag him down. Having his legs pulled out from under him, Dad slid back down the hill, but so did we. Virgil and I struggled to get up and start climbing the hill again before Dad had his wits about him. We thought we were beating him, but he was just toying with us. Just as we started to make headway, Dad reached up with his long, strong arms, grabbed us each by the back of the snow pants and flung us off the hill and into the snow drifts on either side of the pile like we were bags of feed. Once we caught our breath again, all three of us raced up the snow pile from different directions. Dad reached the top first and declared himself King of the Mountain. While he was busy surveying his kingdom, Virgil and I pushed him from behind. As he fell though, Dad twisted around and grabbed my arm, taking me with him, rolling down the hill. Dad and I lay at the foot of the snow pile and laughed as we watched Virgil do his King of the Mountain victory dance.

"Okay, break's over," Dad said as he got up and helped brush snow off of me. "Time to get back at it. Have fun, but no tunnels 'til I get home, ya hear?"

"Got it, Dad."

"Thanks for the pile, Jake," Virgil yelled.

"Sure thing, Kid." He leapt back up on the loader and headed down the road towards the great grandparents', plowing the snow as he went.

We weren't allowed to dig tunnels in the snow pile unless Dad was home and paying attention because they could collapse and trap us. We could dig open air ditches or pits to act as forts though. Dad had made us a great snow pile that wasn't tall and narrow like most snow piles, but rather, tall and still wide at the top. Because it was so majestic, we decided to build a castle at the top of our mountain. We used a spade we found in the garage to dig a hole in the middle of the top of the pile wide enough for us both to sit inside out of the wind. The shoveling was hard work, even taking turns. Once the hole was a few feet deep, I went and asked Mom for a couple of empty ice cream pails and an old milk jug full of water. At that point, we both got inside the hole and continued to dig it deeper, only we used the pails to scoop the snow and instead of tossing the snow over the side, we packed the snow in the pail then flipped it over on the edge of the hole like a round block. Once we had several blocks around the edge, we splashed water on them so they would ice over and solidify. We piled our blocks a few high all around the hole, leaving an open space for a doorway, then dug the doorway ditch to the edge of the mountain and kicked steps into the side down to the bottom. We found an old piece of plywood in the barn and laid it across the top of our block walls for a roof. We stuffed all the cracks with snow and sealed them with water. It was a fine castle for a fine mountain, but we were exhausted, wet, and cold and needed hot chocolate like we needed air to breathe.

Mom had been monitoring our progress from the kitchen window and had already started the milk warming. We tumbled into the mudroom, shedding layers of wet hats, mittens, scarves, parkas, boots, and snow pants into a big, sloppy pile.

"Hang up your jackets and pants and lay your hats and mittens on the radiator or they'll never dry," Mom hollered.

We did as she said, then plopped down at the kitchen table.

Mom made exceptional hot chocolate with milk and canned Hershey's Chocolate Syrup, complete with marshmallows. It was sweet, rich, creamy, and hot and you could literally feel its warmth spreading through your chest, down to your stomach, as you swallowed it. Virgil and I sat and savored it as we dripped. We wore boots and snow pants, but snow and ice somehow always collected on the bottom several inches of the legs of our jeans. Our thawing jeans dripped water on the floor and our thawing bodies dripped water from our noses. Once we started warming up, it felt like life couldn't get much better.

People were still digging out all over the county and no one knew how far the roads would be passable, so no one ventured too far from home. Virgil's birthday party had to be postponed until Saturday, but I walked across the street for supper with his family. I was too excited to give him his present to wait almost a week for the party and besides, we forgot to talk about my mystery.

Virgil and I loved music and listened to it whenever we could. The spring before, Virgil boosted an AM transistor radio from his sister that looked like a ladybug. Its eyes were the volume and tuning controls and when you played it, its wings spread out like it was flying. We listened to it all the time and always kept it with us. Virgil would tie the strap to his belt loop when were on the move.

Virgil's sisters also belonged to a record club, so they got new 45s every month. Whenever we knew they'd be gone for the afternoon, we listened to all of their records, being careful to put them all back in the same order we found them so the girls would never be the wiser.

At Thanksgiving, Virgil's cousin, Jimmy, who lived in the city and had access to all kinds of neat stuff we didn't, gave Virgil one of his old albums, *Led Zeppelin II* released in 1969. We played the album over and over and over until Virgil's mom yelled, "For Pete's sake, would you please stop that racket? You're going to make my ears bleed."

We liked the nearly forbidden flavor of the loud, crashing, manic rock sound, but my favorite song was the mellow *What Is and What Should Never Be*:

And if I say to you tomorrow, take my hand, child, come with me. It's to a castle I will take you, where what's to be, they say will be. Catch the wind, see us spin, sail away, leave today, way up high in the sky. But the wind won't blow, you really shouldn't go. It only goes to show, that you will be mine, by takin' our time. And if you say to me tomorrow, oh what fun it all would be, then what's to stop us, pretty baby, but what is and what should never be? So if you wake up with the sunrise and all your dreams are still as new and happiness is what you need so bad, girl, the answer lies with you.

The lyrics made me daydream and spin fairytales in my head.

The song *Moby Dick* was instrumental only and featured an extended solo by drummer John Bonham. Virgil became obsessed with being a drummer like "Bonzo". He used wooden spoons and practiced on every hard surface he could find to whack.

To help in the pursuit of his dream, I asked Mom to take me with her into the city to the big music store downtown where we went every year to buy the books for my piano lessons. The store was a musical wonderland with every kind of instrument you could think of hanging on the walls and sitting on the shelves and I knew they would have what I needed.

Though I loved Mrs. Sinclair's meatloaf and mashed potatoes, I couldn't wait for supper to be over so Virgil could open his presents. I wrapped mine in a big box stuffed with crumpled up newspapers so he couldn't figure out what it was beforehand. It looked big and with all the newspapers, it only made a little bit of a thump when you shook it. He shredded the wrapping paper and ripped open the box, but then stopped as it looked like just a bunch of newspaper.

"Well what are ya waitin' for? Keep digging," I encouraged.

Virgil tossed balls of newspaper all over the livingroom until he got to the very bottom of the box where he found a long roll of paper. He stood up, held one end, and let it unroll to the floor where out fell a set of real, professional drum sticks.

"What do you think?" I asked.

"They're great," Virgil replied as he stroked them.

"Mom took me to the music store in Aberdeen special to find them. The man there helped me pick them out. I told him I needed the 'longest, heaviest trees' he had, just like Bonzo uses. He was kind of old, so I'm not sure if he knew what I meant. He asked me what kind of drums you played, but when I said you didn't actually have any real drums yet, he told me those were the sticks you needed. They're made out of an oak tree and they're the hardest to break of any of the sticks they had in the store," I said.

"They're way cool, Squirt. Thank you," Virgil said. Virgil was the youngest of four kids and his sisters and brother never called him by his name, but always some word that meant little or small. He didn't like that part of being the youngest, mostly because he didn't have anyone younger to call names himself. I was small for my age and I didn't mind, so I told him it was okay for him to call me little names. Of the large selection he heard routinely, he decided "Squirt" was the one that fit me best, so it was what he almost always called me.

"Let's go try them out," he said. We gathered his drum set from all over the house. It included buckets, boxes, pans, a cookie tin, and an empty oatmeal container. We headed to his room where he set up his drums and I settled into my usual spot in the beanbag chair by the door.

"We have a real live mystery on our hands, Virg," I said.

"We do?"

"Yep. We have to figure it out using nothing but clues, just like Encyclopedia Brown." Virgil didn't like to read all that much, he was more of a doer than a reader, but he did like it if I read books out lout to him and then we acted them out or made up our own stories from there. Encyclopedia Brown, "America's Sherlock Holmes in sneakers," was our favorite.

"What's the mystery?"

"I was stuck out in the blizzard and I can't remember what happened or how I got home."

"For real?"

"Yep."

"Well, we have to start with the facts. What's the last thing you do remember?"

"Um, I went upstairs to get my special sledding mittens, you know, the ones with the leather patches."

"Uh huh. Then what?"

"Then I grabbed the sled and headed out."

"Where did you go?"

"The hill beside the old Nagle farmhouse. I remember it was snowing really hard and the wind started to blow before I got to the stop sign. After that, everything's kind of fuzzy. The next thing I remember for sure I was in my bed and my head hurt."

"You don't remember anything in the middle?"

"Not really."

"Are you sure? Even kinda fuzzy stuff?"

"Well, I keep seeing a floating, green eyeball in my head."

"A floating eyeball? Just one?"

"Uh huh."

"Weird."

"Yeah."

"Where's your sled?"

I sat up at that question. "Oh, Man. I don't know. I didn't think about it, but I'm pretty sure I haven't seen it since then."

"We'll look for it tomorrow. It's evidence. It should have clues. Or maybe not knowing where it is is a clue," Virgil said. "Okay, I'm ready to test out my sticks. Hit the LZ, Squirt."

"Got it."

We rocked out until Mrs. Sinclair banged on the door and said it was time for me to go home and for her to have some blessed peace and quiet before she pulled her hair out.

School wasn't cancelled the next day, just a two hour late start to give the buses extra time, in case they got stuck.

After school, Virgil and I stopped at Bert's for a chat and a Cherry Up.

Bert's was pretty much our favorite place in the world. The official name on the side of the building was Coteau Sundries, but everyone always called it either The Drugstore or Bert's. Bert's was a wonderous place filled with candy, comic books, and everything you could ever need, from cough drops and bandaids to birthday cards, baby bottles, hula hoops, pop guns, and jewelry.

The bell over the door jingled as we walked in, signaling our arrival. We dropped our book bags and parkas on the floor with a thunk, jumped up on the stools at the soda fountain, and pushed ourselves from the counter to spin around and around in circles on the stools until Bert arrived from the back room.

"What'll ya have, kids?" asked Bert as he washed his hands at the sink and flipped the towel over his shoulder.

"Just the usual, Bert," I replied. Our usual was a tall, frosty Cherry Up, heavy on the cherry.

"Coming right up," Bert said as he got the frost covered, heavy glass mugs out of the cooler, pulled a big lever to fill them with 7 Up drawn from the fountain, added a stream of cherry syrup from a tall, skinny bottle with a flourish, stirred them up with a big, shiny, metal swizzle stick, then slid them down the length of the counter so we could reach out and catch the mugs before they slid past us. He only did that if we were the only kids in the store at the time as that could get messy with inexperienced catchers.

We sucked the foam off the top, then un-wrapped our straws and settled in to visit with Bert.

"So I heard you got yourself in a little trouble the other night, Missy," Bert directed his gaze at me.

"Yeah, I guess," I replied. That was the thing about living in a very small town, word spread like wildfire. Everyone knew everything you did, almost before you did it. If we got in trouble in school, we would get fussed at by half a dozen people as we passed the drugstore, the bank, the

THE ROAD HOME

grocery store, the post office, the gas station, you name it. There was no hope of our parents not finding out what we'd done.

"You could've been killed being out in a blizzard like that. Haven't you heard of The Schoolchildren's Blizzard?" Bert said.

"Nuh uh," replied Virgil.

"Tell us the story, Bert," I said.

"Well, it happened on almost the very same day, eighty-seven years ago. All the school buildings were out in the country then, you know, like the little one that sits out in the pasture near the Schmidt farm."

"Yeah, we know where that's at," Virgil said. "There's still a desk in there with a really cool drawing somebody carved on the top."

"On January 11, 1888, the morning was sunny and unseasonably warm, so kids walked to that very school and ones just like it all over Iowa, Nebraska, and Dakota Territory in their shirtsleeves and good shoes. It was so warm, they left their coats, mittens, and boots at home and skipped the couple of miles to school, happy as you please. Along about afternoon recess, the kids saw sundogs in the sky."

"Hey, we did too," I piped up.

"Well, sure you did. You almost always catch sundogs just before a hard blizzard comes."

"Because the sled full of snow tips over," I nodded sagely.

"So they say. Well, a few of the teachers in those schools knew that too. They kept a stray eye on the sky and started sending the kids home as soon as the heavy clouds moved in. That storm was a real bad one though and it hit like a clap of thunder. Just like that," Bert snapped his fingers, "the temperature dropped like a rock, falling more than sixty degrees before they could even get out the door. As soon as the kids started out on the path towards home,

33

the sky opened up and dumped snow so heavy and thick you couldn't see your hand in front of your face."

"Wow," sighed Virgil.

"Oh, no," I fretted, "What did the kids do?"

"What could they do but try to keep going and get home as fast as they could? Problem was, that blizzard hit like a tornado, the wind blowing all that snow something fierce. It was a white out. They couldn't see a darn thing and some of them got confused and turned around. The ones who couldn't find any shelter and didn't run into a fence or anything they could follow to find their way, just wandered about in the snow until they dropped in their tracks and froze to death."

Virgil and I sat in stunned and sober silence as Bert continued.

"By morning, more than two hundred children lay dead on the prairie."

"Two hundred?" I breathed, as a tear slipped from the corner of my eye.

"More than. It was devastating for the entire region. Word of the tragedy quickly spread throughout the country and the steady stream of settlers stopped right quick as the Great Plains became known as a place where blizzards kill children on their way home from school. Living in this land has never been easy or a pursuit for the faint of heart," Bert concluded.

"Dad says it keeps the riff raff out because crooks don't like their living hard," I said.

"Could be," Bert agreed.

We polished off our Cherry Ups, grabbed a couple penny pieces of Bazooka chewing gum, asked Bert to put it on our parents' tabs, thanked him for the story, and continued on our way home. We had to get home before dark to find my sled and look for clues to solve the mystery of the missing day and the floating eye.

four

Of the many mystery-solving kids to be found in books, like the Boxcar Children, the Hardy Boys, Trixie Belden, and Nancy Drew, Encyclopedia Brown was by far our favorite. A lot of the other stories seemed far-fetched to us and unlikely to happen in a real kid's life and the characters were a little hokey as well. Encyclopedia Brown seemed more like a regular kid and I liked that his sidekick, Sally Kimball, wasn't a prissy, girlie girl, but rather was uncharacteristically the muscle in the partnership as she was "Idaville's best fighter under twelve years of age" and Encyclopedia's bodyguard. Encyclopedia stories could actually happen. They were short, sweet, and to the point, without a lot of extra information you didn't need to know and they were interactive, which made them really fun to read together like Virgil and I did. Each book had ten different mysteries to solve and it was up to the reader to solve them before looking for the answer in the back of the book, so of course we had a contest going regarding who could come up with the correct solution first. I was a better reader, but Virgil was a better mystery solver.

For the first time ever, we had a real mystery to solve and we weren't trying to invent one where none existed. We soon discovered however, that finding clues to solve a mystery was a lot harder than reading and recognizing clues in a story already written. We weren't quite sure where to start. We sat in our snow mountain castle to come up with a battle plan.

"Okay. One more time, what's the last thing you remember for sure?" Virgil asked.

"I left the house with my sled and headed for the hill beside the Nagle farmhouse," I replied.

"And what's the next thing you remember?"

"Waking up in bed with Mom."

"How did you get there?"

"I'm not exactly sure, but Mom said she found me in the mudroom asleep on Dad's coveralls."

"Did you find your sled?"

"No. We need to look around again, but I haven't seen it and I don't really want to tell Mom and Dad that I lost it until I'm really sure that I did. They'll freak out. It's only a few weeks old."

"Okay. We'll look around the yard real good and then try to retrace your steps if we don't find it."

"Got it."

Virgil stuck his right hand in front of him, I slapped my right hand on top of his, then Virgil's left, then my left, we bobbed the pile of hands up and down three times, and yelled, "Let's go!" just like the high school basketball boys did it.

We searched all over the yard, but didn't see the sled anywhere and any tracks it could have made had long been filled in with fresh snow.

"Well, that was a bust. We'll have to move on to Plan B," said Virgil.

"Plan B?" I asked.

"Yeah, retrace your steps. Plan A was to find the sled in the yard."

"Oh, right, Plan B. After I went upstairs and got my mittens, I picked up my sled, which was leaning up against the house outside the back door, and headed for the Nagle hill."

"Street or ditch?"

"Street. The snow in the ditch was already pretty deep."

We walked down the street toward the Nagle farm.

"Which way did you go up the hill?"

"Well, that's the thing, I started out going right up the middle, thinking it would be far enough away from the boulder near the mailbox side, but it's steeper than I remembered, the snow was slippery, and it was getting hard to see, so I kinda had to zigzag and by the time I got to the top, the wind was blowing. Everything was just white and I couldn't tell where I was. I was at the top of the hill, but I couldn't see the road, the boulder, the mailbox, a fence post, nuthin'. I didn't want to walk back, so I just jumped on the sled and headed down."

"Did you go down on your butt or your belly?"

"Belly."

"Pro'ly not your best plan."

"Probably not. I just thought maybe it wouldn't be so windy down low to the ground."

"Do you remember seeing a car or a truck or anything?"

"Nuh uh."

We trudged up the hill, looking from side to side for tracks or unusual lumps. We looked all around the top of the hill then looked to see what we could see from the top, wondering who else could have seen me.

"Nothing is close enough but the Nagle farmhouse and there's nobody there."

"Are you sure?"

"Pretty sure. Mr. Nagle died last spring while he was planting, remember? Mrs. Nagle passed on at Thanksgiving."

"I guess it had to be somebody going by then."

"I don't think any strangers would be on this side of town. If somebody drove past and stopped to help me, we would have heard about it by now, wouldn't we?"

"You'd think."

"Now what?"

"Well, you had to've hit something with your head to get that goose egg. Let's look for that."

We zigzagged back and forth down the hill, shuffling our feet under the blanket of snow, checking for anything hidden I might have hit.

"I guess you must've hit the boulder. I don't see anything else."

"Me neither."

We shuffled our feet all around the boulder, then brushed the snow off of it, and looked it over top to bottom.

"Look! There it is," Virgil exclaimed.

"There what is?" I asked.

"A clue."

"Where?"

"Right here, see, red paint and a scratch in the rock."

"It is a clue, a real live clue. I must have hit the rock with the runners on my sled."

"And with your head. I guess it knocked you out."

"Wow."

"Now we know what happened. We just have to figure out where your sled is and who helped you."

Just then, the whistle on the water tower blew, meaning it was 6:00 p.m. and time for supper.

"Shoot. We're late." Virgil said. "If I don't get to the table in the next five minutes, there won't be anything left."

"You can come eat at my house. Julie's too little to eat much before we get there."

"What're ya havin'?"

"I don't know, but it's usually pretty good and it's better than the nothing you'll get if you're late. C'mon, we can call your mom from the house."

"'Kay."

"Make sure the door is closed and don't track," Mom yelled, as we crashed through the back door. "Are you staying for supper, Virgil?"

"Please?"

"Call your mom and make sure it's okay. Set the table, Jennie."

"What are we having?" I asked.

"You're eating whatever shows up," Dad said as he came in the kitchen, kissed the top of Mom's head, and washed his hands with dishsoap.

"Mom says if I'm any trouble, send me home." Virgil said as he hung up the phone.

"Mmm. Sloppy joes and fried potatoes. We're starving."

"What did you eat at school?" Dad asked as we all sat down.

"Chipped beef gravy on toast and tator tots," I groaned.

"They're still making that? We called that sh—"

"Jake," Mom cut him off with her warning tone, but Virgil knew what he was going to say.

"Yeah, we call it that too." Mom turned her one raised eyebrow on Virgil who cleared his throat and said, "Ah, they still make it…a lot. And the lunch ladies won't let you have seconds on tator tots unless your gravy is gone either."

"You could only have one cookie too."

"Life's tough all over," Dad said. "What were you two up to this afternoon?"

"Looking for clues," I said.

"To what?"

"A mystery," Virgil replied.

"I got that much, Kid," Dad said and Virgil grinned. Dad didn't figure he was going to get anything but smart aleck responses from us, so he left it at that and started a conversation with Mom.

"Took me all afternoon to get that damn loader fixed. That thing is such a piece of…" Mom's right eyebrow went up again and Dad stopped mid-sentence. "Don't cuss, kids, mothers don't like it." We giggled and then everyone chewed in silence for a couple of minutes.

"Who owns the Nagle farm now that Mr. and Mrs. Nagle are gone?" Virgil asked.

"Well, I guess Bud Nagle does," Dad replied.

"Who's that?" I asked.

"Mr. and Mrs. Nagle's son," Dad said.

"I didn't know they had a son."

"Sure they did. I guess maybe he was gone before you were old enough to remember him though."

"Gone where?"

"Vietnam."

Virgil and I looked at each other and slowly stopped chewing. We didn't know a whole lot about the war in Vietnam, but we saw the news on TV. We knew enough to know it was bad, that the scenes always looked smoky and dirty, and that lots of people died there.

"Was he a soldier?" I whispered.

"Yep. I believe he left college and volunteered without waiting to be drafted."

"Is he still alive?"

"Far as I know. Haven't heard otherwise."

"He was a senior when I moved here as a freshman," Mom said. "He was so handsome. He was the quarterback on the football team, Homecoming King, captain of the basketball team, broke all kinds of records in track, he was something else. All the girls in school thought he was just dreamy, but he never dated anyone seriously. I don't think he had time. In addition to all of the sports, he helped out on the farm and got really good grades too. He planned to become a doctor."

Dad made that "pashht" noise that meant he was disgusted, disbelieving, or irritated. Grandma Cori hated the "pashht" noise. She said it was like all the cuss words in the world rolled into one noise. When she heard it, her nostrils flared as she sucked in a deep breath through her nose to calm down. The "pashht" noise was a family thing. Dad got it from Papa and Papa got it from Great Grandma Sophie. I wasn't sure who Great Grandma Sophie got it from, but I thought it possible that a long, long ago, genius ancestor from the old country invented the "pashht" noise, a super colossal cuss word that you could say without getting in trouble because no one could prove that you'd actually used a bad word.

We giggled as Mom smiled and Dad scowled.

"Thank you for supper, Mrs. Ericson," Virgil said on his way out the door.

"You can call me Trish, Virgil. Mrs. Ericson is my mother-in-law."

Virgil just nodded. "I'll catch you in the morning, Squirt. See ya."

"Wouldn't wanna be ya," I replied with a grin.

five

When I got home from school the next day, my sled was by the back door. I ran back around the house yelling for Virgil. "Look, it's my sled."

Virgil started inspecting it for clues.

"Remember the paint on the rock? Look here, there are brush marks in the paint on the runners. I think it was spray painted before. And see around this rivet? It's a little brighter color. I think somebody repainted the runners International Harvester red," said Virgil.

"The rock was scratched too. I must've hit it with the fender or the runners."

"Yep. There's just a little bit of a ripple here on the edge of the front fender where somebody pounded out a dent."

"Who could it have been?"

"You know, I was thinkin' on that today. I think it was Bud Nagle."

"But he hasn't been here for years."

"I think he's here now."

I looked toward the Nagle farmhouse. "It doesn't look like anybody is home to me."

"Meet me in the castle. I'll be right back."

When Virgil came back, he had his dad's hunting binoculars.

"We need to do surveillance."

"What's that?"

"Watch. Look around. Wait and see if we see any signs of movement. Like a stakeout on _Kojak_." Virgil reached in his pocket, pulled out two suckers with looped sticks from our bank sucker stash, handed me the purple one, stuck the red one in his mouth, then pulled it out and said, "Who loves you, Baby?" in his best Telly Savalas voice.

I rolled my eyes and said, "I think I'd rather pretend it was a stakeout on _Police Woman_. Sergeant Pepper Anderson always gets to wear a disguise."

"What are you going to be disguised as to spy on a farmhouse? A cow?"

"Hardy har har, Lippy. Look through the binoculars. What do you see?"

"Just the usual so far. Wait. I think there might be tire tracks near the garage."

"Really?"

"Looks like it. I don't see anything coming out of the chimney though. Must be cold in there."

"He could have an electric space heater."

"Maybe."

We took turns watching the house through the binoculars until our knees started to freeze and it started getting dark, but didn't see any other signs of life.

Our suspicions were confirmed when Dad came home that evening.

"I heard at the gas station that Bud Nagle finally came home."

"Really?" Mom said. "Where has he been all this time? Is he okay?"

"Nobody seems to know. Looks like he got pretty banged up though. They almost didn't recognize him."

I couldn't wait to tell Virgil the news. The mystery might be solved.

The next day was Saturday and we planned to meet at our lilac bush fort on the edge of the yard at 10:30, after all the good cartoons were over.

"Virgil, guess what."

"Chicken butt."

"No, Dork, I'm serious. You were right. Bud Nagle is back. He must've been the one who saved me in the blizzard. We have to go see him."

Virgil looked toward the dark, silent house. "Are you sure he wants company?"

"We're kids, not company."

Virgil followed me with a shrug. He knew there was no sense arguing with me when I had made up my mind.

We trudged up the front porch steps, opened the screen door with a screech, pounded on the storm door, then waited. Nothing. Virgil shielded his eyes with his hands and pressed his nose up against the window glass trying to see beyond the lace curtains. I took my mittens off and pounded on the door again with my bare knuckles so the knock wasn't muffled. Still nothing.

"You know, this door is for company. I bet he's using the back door by the garage."

We went around back to the kitchen door and both banged on it without mittens so he'd be sure to hear us. A couple of minutes passed without a response, so we really threw ourselves into pounding on the door one last time. The door flung open so quickly and with such force that we both tumbled through the doorway, then someone roared, "What!"

When I looked up at the source of the bellow, I couldn't stop myself from letting out a squeak of surprise and fright. A broad shouldered man towered above us with inky black hair sticking out in all directions, a full beard, and an angry look in his red-rimmed, green eye.

"One eye!" I exclaimed to Virgil.

"Get out!" yelled the man.

"You only have one eye," I said to the man.

"Get out now," the man growled.

"I couldn't remember what happened to me in the snowstorm, but I remembered one green eye floating near my face. It must have been you. Thank you so much, Mister," I said as I wrapped my arms around his waist, pressing my cheek against his stomach.

The man stood in stunned silence.

I stood back and said, "I'm Jennie Ericson, Jennie with an 'ie', not a 'y', and this is my best friend, Virgil Sinclair. Virgil just turned nine on Monday, but his birthday party isn't until this afternoon because of the blizzard. I'll be nine the end of May. We're your neighbors. We live across the street from each other right over there. My parents are Jake and Trish Ericson, maybe you know them? You're Bud Nagle, right? Mom said you were older so maybe you don't remember them, but they remember you."

The man didn't respond.

"I guess you don't talk much, huh? That's okay. Grandma Mae says Virg and I could talk the hind legs off a donkey. Doesn't she say that, Virg?"

"Yep."

"I don't know what that means, do you, Virgil?"

"Nope. Sometimes she says we talk her ear off. That makes sense, but I don't get the donkey leg thing."

"Anyway, we talk a lot, so it's okay if you don't like to talk. We don't mind."

"Aren't you scared?" asked the man.

"Of what?"

"Me."

"Of course not, Silly. You saved my life. Why would you hurt me now? We came to say thank you. We solved the mystery. We figured out that you must be the one who saved me from freezing to death in the blizzard when I bonked my head and knocked myself out and you fixed my sled too, so thank you. I owe you big time."

"You screamed."

"I was just surprised is all. You're big, dark, and hairy. My dad is big, but he's not dark or hairy. He's blonde like us. You were scary in the dark like that for a minute."

"Oh, you mean, 'cause of the one eye thing?" said Virgil. "It doesn't scare us. I think it's cool. It makes you look like a pirate."

"Yeah, it's way cool. Hey, it makes you look like Rooster Cogburn. Have you seen that movie? It was just on TV a few weeks ago. What was it called, Virgil?"

"*True Grit.*"

"Right. *True Grit* with John Wayne. It was a great movie. Dad loves The Duke. We watch all of his movies when they come on TV. *The Searchers* used to be my favorite, you know, when they look for the girl kidnapped by the Indians? Then *McClintock* was my favorite because his red-haired wife was kind of funny when she yelled at him and he tried to spank her, but now my all-time favorite forever is *True Grit*. It works out just perfect. Since you already have an eye patch, you can obviously be Rooster Cogburn. I'll be Mattie Ross, of course. I really like her. She's spunky. And Virgil can be that La Beef guy, which is great because Virgil really, really likes Glen Campbell. Glen Campbell is the guy who pretends to be La Beef in the movie, but in real life he's a singer and he plays guitar. He used to have his own show on TV and sometimes he was on *The Smothers Brothers*. I like those guys. They're funny. Don't worry, Virgil, we won't let you die like La Beef does in the movie. Wait, does he really die? I'm not sure. They sort of make it look like he dies because you don't see him at the very end, but I'm not sure if he really died or not. Either way, you won't die in our version, Virgil."

Bud just stared at us with a sort of puzzled expression.

"Are you back for good?" asked Virgil.

"For awhile," said Bud.

"Mom said you left before I was old enough to remember you. What took you so long to come home?" I asked.

"Yeah, what took you so long?"

"I got lost."

"You couldn't remember how to get home?" asked Virgil.

"There are a lot of ways to get lost," Bud replied.

"Are you going to farm?" I asked.

"A little."

"You have a lot of work to do then," declared Virgil.

"We can help," I said. "Did you know that some people, I don't remember what people, but some people in a different place, or maybe it was a different time, but this place, like Indians or something, I forget, but anyway, I read that there are some people who believe that if someone saves your life, then you need to spend the rest of your life doing things for that person because you owe them your life. Without the person who saved you, you wouldn't have a life, so you need to spend the life you have serving that person. You saved my life, so I owe you and I'll help you."

"Yeah, me too. Squirt here is my best friend. We share everything. If she owes you, I owe you. We'll both help you. You might think we're just kids, but we can help with lots of stuff."

"Yeah, lots of stuff."

"No thanks," said Bud.

"No really, we want to," I said.

"We have to," said Virgil.

"Thank you, but no," replied Bud.

"Nope. We've decided. We're going to help you. We insist," I said.

"Yeah, we insist," said Virgil.

"Don't bother being polite and saying no. Besides, we'll just wear you down. We're like that. Grandma says we're ten...ten...ah, ten..."

"I thought you said you were nine," said Bud.

"No, no. What are we, Virgil? We're ten..."

"Acious," said Virgil.

"Right. Tenacious. We're tenacious. That means we don't give up or take no for an answer."

"Yeah, you're pretty much stuck with us. C'mon, Squirt, we have to get ready for my birthday party. We'll come by regular like, okay?"

"Later, Bud. We're going to be great friends. You'll see."

As we walked down the driveway, I heard Bud say, "You're gonna be trouble, Baby Sister." I laughed and yelled back, "I told you you'd be a great Rooster Cogburn."

six

By the following Saturday, we had yet to see Bud outside or even any signs that he lived there. Everyone else was curious as well. There had never been so much traffic on our road. There isn't a whole lot of entertainment in a small town in the middle of nowhere, especially in the winter. You can't do much farming or much of anything else in the snow and cold, so lots of folks just sit around wondering what everyone else is doing and gossiping. Gossiping requires at least a kernel of information to start however, so though the entire population for miles around had heard through the grapevine that Bud Nagle was back, not too many people had actually seen him, and kernels of information for the gossip gristmill to grind were few and far between.

I told Great Grandma Sophie about my new friend, Bud, when we had my regular, Friday night sleepover.

"You know, they had that boy far too late in life, but they were so tickled. Both of them getting on so in years, people worried the baby'd be touched in the head, but he showed them, he was smart as a whip from day one and he was always a good boy. Though I know he wasn't there for their last days, I'm sure he had good reason. I'm sure as certain none of the rumors these old hens around here have been clucking about are true. Going off to war is a hard thing no matter how you slice it."

"Well, that house is going to need a good airing out if he's to stay there. It's been closed up for a couple of months now and you know poor Elaine wasn't doing well for several months before she passed on. I'm sure it needs a good scrubbing all over. You see he takes care of that, you hear? Elaine would be fit to be tied if she knew people were coming by day and night and might see the place a mess. Rolling in her grave," Great Grandma muttered.

When I went home, I stopped by Virgil's and told him we needed to go help Bud clean.

"Clean?" Virgil groaned, "What for?"

"Great Grandma Sophie says poor Mrs. Nagle will be rolling in her grave if we don't make sure the house is ship shape with all these people driving by trying to look in." I cast a wary eye to the side of Virgil's house toward the United Methodist Cemetery across the field where I feared Mrs. Nagle had already started rolling.

"Criminy."

"Don't cuss. Meet me after lunch and bring your mom's feather duster. We don't have one of those."

"Fine," Virgil sighed with an air of resignation.

As I sat on the floor to tug off my boots, I hollered to Mom, "Where's the mop bucket?"

"What?" Mom called from kitchen.

"Where's the mop bucket?"

"There's an ice cream pail by the dryer."

"No, I need the mop bucket with the wheels," I said as I came in the kitchen.

"My mop bucket with the wheels is for cleaning, not for whatever idea you have in that pretty, little head of yours."

"I need it for cleaning."

"Really?" Mom asked with one eyebrow arched clear up in the middle of her forehead.

"Yes, really."

"Cleaning what?"

"A friend's house."

"I don't believe I've ever seen you use it to clean this house. Do you know how to use it properly?"

"Yes," I said with a dramatic sigh and roll of my eyes.

"I tell you what, you show me you know how to use my bucket and cleaning supplies by cleaning up that mess of an entryway and you can borrow them all you like as long they are returned in the same condition and place where you found them."

"But it's a mudroom. It's supposed to be dirty. You know, it's the room where we keep the mud."

Mom just looked at me with that darn raised eyebrow, which meant she'd laid down the law and arguing was a waste of time.

"Ugh. Fine," I said with a pout and stomped off to hang up all the jackets and hats, pair up all the mittens and gloves, line up the boots and shoes along the wall, straighten the rugs, and sweep and mop the floor.

Virgil and I showed up on Bud's doorstep loaded down with our supplies, ready to do battle with his messy house. We pounded on the door.

"Go away," we heard from inside.

"It's not nosy neighbors. It's Jennie and Virgil. Let us in," I called.

"No. Go. A. Way."

"Now, Bud. Don't be that way. You know you like us. We're here to help," I said.

"C'mon, Bud. It's colder than a well digger's butt out here," said Virgil.

"Virgil, watch your mouth," I giggled.

"I did watch my mouth. Butt's not the word Dad uses when he says that."

The door opened as Bud said, "What?"

We bustled through the door with our cleaning supplies and took off our hats, gloves, and parkas, hanging them on the kitchen chairs.

"Well, just make yourselves at home, why don't you?"

"Thanks," I chirped.

Bud shook his head.

"We came to help you clean the house."

"Huh?" asked Bud.

"Yeah, that's what I said," grumbled Virgil.

"Great Grandma Sophie says your house needs to be aired out and scrubbed down. It's what your mom would want."

Bud just stared at me.

I took one of Dad's bandanas out of the back pocket of my overalls and started tying it around my head like a scarf. "Empty the bucket and find a broom, Virg."

"Yes, Bossy Pants."

"The house is fine," Bud declared.

"Fine? It's dark as a badger hole in here. How can you tell?" I said as I started pulling down on the dark green window shades to make them roll up with a snap and a cloud of dust that shimmered in the sudden sunlight as it floated through the air.

"Whoa, Man. This place is a dump. You been living in just this room?" Virgil asked as he looked around the kitchen at the empty bottles and cans, dirty dishes, and blankets on the floor next to the space heater.

Bud just turned his scowl on Virgil and crossed his arms.

"Mmm, mmm, mmm. Your momma sure would be fit to be tied," I said as I shook my head and started pushing a kitchen chair up to the sink so I could reach the faucet to start the dishes. "Well, don't just stand there. Find a garbage bag and start picking up this mess," I ordered Bud, who still stood in silence.

"When she gets bossy like this, Man, it's a lot less hassle to just do what she says 'til she winds down," said Virgil. "She'll get bored and move on to something else that might be more fun in a little bit."

Bud stood and watched us a few more minutes, then ran his hand through his hair, sighed, and started opening cupboard doors looking for a garbage bag.

After cleaning, scrubbing, and dusting for several hours, much longer than Virgil anticipated my attention span would allow, I declared the house fit as a fiddle, as Grandma Mae would say. "Now, Bud, you need to start living in the whole house like you're supposed to. Virgil's dad knows the guy who drives the heating oil truck. We'll tell him to stop by just as soon as he can. They won't let anybody freeze to death. I'm pretty sure they'll let you pay on account if you need to. We'll be back after school in a couple of days to see how's it going. And don't close all the window shades again. No sunshine is just depressing. Besides, see how pretty the light and shadows look on the wall when the sun shines through the lace curtains? Everybody needs a little pretty in their lives, even boys. Later, Alligator."

Bud just stood holding the door open as we drug our junk out onto the driveway. I stopped and turned, "You're supposed to say, 'After while, Crocodile'."

Bud cocked his head with a quizzical look in his one green eye.

"Oh, Bud. We're going to have to work on you," I sighed.

"Yeah, Man. Lighten up," said Virgil as we trundled down the driveway towards home.

seven

On February 2, 1975, Mom and I watched Dorothy Hamill win her second United States Figure Skating Championship. When her performance was over, we both sighed and clapped our hands. It was the prettiest thing. She looked so graceful, gliding, spinning, and twirling over the ice. I was inspired.

The next Saturday, I told Virgil we needed to go ice skating. We emptied our book bags, loaded up our stuff, and headed over to Bud's house.

Bud greeted us at the door with a resigned, "Hey, Little Sister. What do you want today?"

Undaunted by his lack of enthusiasm, I said, "We want to go ice skating, but it's really windy. Can we use your stock dam? It's the only one around going the right direction." Stock dams were big holes dug in pastures to try to hold water for cattle to drink. Usually, they were dug along a dry draw or low spot in the hopes that rainwater runoff would collect there and fill it up. When the stock dams were dug, the dirt that was dug up was piled on either side of the draw. Both because, well, what else would you do with a bunch of dirt in the middle of a pasture, but also, because the dirt piles would block the wind coming from those two directions and provide the cattle with a little shelter.

"I guess. Your folks know where you are?"

"Oh, sure," I said, but then a thought struck me, Bud needed to have a little fun. "But we can't go that far without an adult, so we need you to come with us."

"I don't know."

"Please, please, puh-leeeeeeeze," I begged as I hung on his arm and batted my eyelashes up at him in what I hoped was a pleading and endearing look.

"I don't have any ice skates," Bud replied.

"Oh neither do we," piped Virgil. "We're cowboy skating."

"Cowboy skating?"

"Yeah, didn't you ever do that as a kid?" asked Virgil.

"Ah…"

"Those'll work," Virgil declared as he pointed to a beat up pair of cowboy boots on the rug next to the door. He stuck the boots in his bag and we both started tugging on Bud's hands.

"C'mon, Bud. It'll be fun. I promise. We won't stay long. Pretty please with sugar on top?" I asked as I reached up on tiptoe and pulled on his shirt collar to get his face down low enough to kiss his scarred cheek and beam my highest wattage smile at him.

Bud's green eye stared at me through his thick, dark lashes as he touched a finger to the spot I'd just kissed then he shook his head and grumbled, "Okay. Half an hour. That's it."

"Yay!" we cheered as we scrambled back out the door with Bud grudgingly bringing up the rear.

When we got out to stock dam, we just stood behind the dirt piles for a few minutes and savored the lack of wind buffeting us about. Then Virgil and I plopped down on the ground and started tugging off our snow boots and pulling on our cowboy boots. We ran through the snow and frozen mud on the edge of the dam before leaping on the ice, sliding until our momentum ran out. We went opposite directions, then turned around and tried to slide into each other, falling down in a giggling tangle of arms and legs.

Bud watched us for a few minutes, then muttered, "What the hell," and sat down to switch out his boots too.

"I need your help, Bud!" I yelled.

"What?" he replied as he stepped gingerly onto the ice.

"I need you to spin me around in a circle by my arm and then let go to kind of fling me out on the ice so I can practice my twirls."

"Twirls?"

"Yes. I need to practice my twirls so I can be a figure skater like Dorothy Hamill."

Virgil started laughing so hard he couldn't stand up straight.

"What's so funny?" I demanded.

"You can't be like Dorothy Hamill," he snorted.

"I can so. Dad said I can be anything I want to be."

"Maybe, if what you want to be just needs brains, but not if it needs coordination."

"Humpf," I huffed, stuck my nose in the air, and daintily held out the hand closest to Bud's good arm with the other fisted on my cocked hip. "Twirl me, Bud."

Bud gently took my hand and slowly turned in a circle.

"No, no," instructed Virgil. "You gotta go a lot faster than that. Really whip her around and then just toss her. She won't break. She's a lot sturdier than she looks. Her dad does it for her all the time. She'll fall down 'cause she's a terrible klutz, but she won't break."

I threw Virgil a scowl for that last crack, but said, "Yeah, go lots faster, Bud."

Bud did as instructed, with me squealing, "Faster, faster," until we were going so fast my feet left the ground, then he let go and I flew through the air. Miraculously, I did land on my feet to slide on the ice, but as soon as I twisted my body around to twirl, my ankles wobbled, my feet and legs tangled up, and I landed on my behind with a thud.

"Uff da!" I exclaimed at the impact.

"Are you okay?" asked Bud.

"She'll shake it off," Virgil declared with a wave of his hand.

I swayed back and forth from the residual dizziness, mentally felt my body for broken bones, then lifted my head with a grin, and said, "Do it again."

We stayed a lot longer than half an hour and headed back to the house tired and sore, with cheeks bright red from both the cold and the exertion. Virgil recounted all our best wipeouts in his sportscaster voice, using my cowboy boot heel for a microphone.

Though he didn't say a word, out of the corner of my eye, I saw Bud smile for the first time since I'd met him and it made my heart glad.

eight

Dad opened the back door, stomped the slush off his boots, and hollered, "Jennie, get dressed. I've got something outside and I need your help."

I ran down the stairs, grabbed the door frame, and slid around the corner in my stocking feet on the kitchen linoleum. "What is it?"

"C'mon outside and see. Hurry up. Wear your snow boots and don't forget your hat."

I jammed on my boots and parka and raced out the door, ducking back in to grab a stocking cap off the hook.

Dad was walking across the yard toward the old garage and I ran to catch up with him.

"What is it?" I asked again.

Dad took my hand in his, leaned down, placed a finger against his lips, and said, "Shhh, now. Quiet. Look here."

We crept into the garage toward the back corner where he'd put a pile of hay. We knelt down next to it and peered over the edge. Curled into a ball was a mound of wet, matted black hide. The ball of black started to shiver and I caught my breath as it lifted its head and turned toward us.

"It's a calf. A really fresh one," I breathed.

"Yep. Hold your hand out to him real slow. Let him smell you."

"It's okay. I won't hurt you, Little Fella. See?" He nuzzled my hand. The top of his nose was the softest thing in the whole world and he had the longest eyelashes I'd ever seen.

"How come you put him in here?" I asked.

"He needs somebody to take care of him until he gets bigger. Know anybody who could do that?"

I giggled. "I could."

"I don't know about that. Are you sure? It's a big job."

"Sure, I'm sure."

"It's a lot of responsibility. He won't make it without a lot of TLC and he might not make it anyway. He's pretty small."

"He can make it. I was pretty small when I was born, but I was a good gainer, right, Dad?"

"That's right, First Born, you were, but this little guy's got extra problems."

"What extra problems?"

"Well, he's blind for one."

"You mean he can't see anything at all?"

"No. Look when he opens his eyes. He doesn't have any pupils or irises. He's pretty sickly. I'm not sure what else might be wrong with him."

"What happened to his momma?"

"Nothing happened to her."

"Then why does he need someone else to take care of him?"

"She won't do it."

"What do you mean she won't do it? Why not?" I demanded.

"She knows he's sick and different from other calves."

"Then she should take extra good care of him. My momma would never not take care of me if I was sickly and different."

"Well, you have a good momma, Baby Girl."

"That cow is a bad momma and she just earned herself a trip to the sale barn, right, Dad?" That's what Dad always said when cattle were being stubborn getting in the shoot or getting out of the fence all the time or just being ornery and aggravating him.

"You think so, huh?"

"Yeah, Dad. We don't want any bad mommas in our herd. You need to sell her."

"Okay then."

"Do you promise?"

"First chance I get, the bad momma's going to the sale barn." Dad kissed my forehead to seal the deal.

"Don't worry, Baby. I'll be your momma now and I'll take good care of you," I told the calf as I held my hand near his nose again. "He needs a blanket, Dad. He's shivering."

"We'll see if Mom's got an old one and get him some warm milk."

"We'll be right back, Baby." As we got up and started walking way, the calf began to beller weakly. "He misses me already, Dad."

Dad smiled down at me and put his hand on top of my head to shake it. He stopped to get a handful of black rubber nipples and a can of milk replacer out of the pickup.

I ran inside hollering, "Mom! We need an old blanket warmed up in the dryer. It's an emergency."

Mom found a ratty old quilt falling apart at the seams and put it in the dryer. Dad started the hot water in the sink and told me to get a few empty pop bottles from the collection in the porch we were saving to redeem at Bert's.

"Find a funnel, Jennie." I found one in the drawer with the measuring cups and put it on the first pop bottle. "Fill it up to about here with the milk replacer powder," Dad said as he held his finger against the bottle.

I spooned the powder in the bottle then Dad filled it with hot water, held his thumb over the open top, and shook it to mix it up. He stretched the rubber nipples over the tops of the bottles and handed them to me. He got the quilt out of the dryer and we headed back out to the garage.

"Approach him quiet and slow or he'll get scared again since he can't see you," Dad said. "Let's try and feed him first before we give him the blanket."

I held the bottle up to the calf's mouth, but he didn't move.

Dad said, "I think we'll have to help him 'til he gets the hang of it." Dad grabbed hold of the calf's jaws and pried his mouth open. The calf started struggling and trying to move away. "Tip the bottle up, squeeze the nipple, and pull down on it to squirt some milk in his mouth," Dad instructed.

The tiny calf choked and sputtered a little, but started swallowing and as he did, Dad slowly let go of his jaws until his mouth was around the nipple. "Move the bottle back and forth a little so he gets the sucking motion down."

The little calf caught on quickly and began sucking on his own. When he got to the end of the bottle, he started head butting my chest looking for more.

"That's good," Dad said. "I was worried he wasn't going to eat. Give him all he'll take."

"See, Dad. He's a good gainer, just like me."

"I think you might be right, Sweet Pea."

After the calf finished all three bottles, Dad put the quilt over him and I lay by his side in the hay and petted his head between his ears.

"Well, what's his name, Momma?" Dad asked me.

I studied the solemn little calf for a few minutes and then proclaimed, "Ajax."

"Ajax?" Dad questioned with a chuckle.

"Yeah. All the letters sound strong and boy-like and I want him to grow up big and strong. Plus, since his eyeballs are all white like that with those little flecks of blue, they look like the laundry detergent does. His eyes are what's different about him. Maybe if his name points out the different thing first, but like he's proud of it, being different won't be such a big deal."

Dad just looked at me for a minute, then rubbed my cheek with his thumb and said, "Maybe so."

"I think he'll be okay now that his tummy is full. You go on inside. It's past your bed time."

"I'm his momma, remember? I need to sleep out here with my baby."

"I don't think your momma would like that much. She's already not going to like that her girl smells like a barn and it's too late for a bath."

"But he's cold and sickly. He needs me to stay warm," I protested.

"I'm going to rig up some heat lamps in here to keep him warm. You'll have to get up early to feed him again before you go to school, so you need to get some sleep in your bed. Go on now."

"Oh, all right," I grumbled. "Thanks for letting me take care of him, Dad. I'll do a good job."

"See that you do."

"'Night, Dad."

"'Night, Baby Girl."

We both gave each other big, smacking kisses on the cheek.

I pulled the quilt up around Ajax's neck, kissed him on the soft spot on the top of his nose, and said, "Sleep tight. Don't let the bed bugs bite."

Dad just shook his head as I gamboled off to the house.

The next morning, Dad hollered up the stairs, "Roll out, Jennie Marie!"

I groaned and covered my head with the blankets. Then I remembered Ajax, threw off the covers, leapt out of bed, jerked on the overalls lying on the floor, grabbed some socks, tucked in my nightgown, and snapped the buckles as I ran down the stairs.

"I can hear your baby crying. You'd better hustle up and get those bottles ready," Dad said.

I turned the hot water on and started putting in the milk replacer powder while Dad poured another cup of coffee. Things were going swell until I tried to mix them the way Dad had. Turns out my thumb was just a little too small to keep a seal on the bottle opening. Just as I got a good shake going, my thumb slipped off the edge and into the hole and milk came spewing out of the bottle...all over Mom as she walked into the kitchen.

Time stopped for half a second, then I gasped, Dad coughed, and Mom screeched through clenched teeth, "What is going on in here?"

We all started speaking at once.

"Sorry, Mom. I was trying to mix up the bottle and..."

"Jake, why are you letting her spray milk all over the kitchen and not..."

"I need to go out and start the truck..."

And Julie started screaming for all she was worth from the other room because she was missing all the action.

Mom closed her eyes and held both sides of her head with her hands. I knew she was counting to ten and I should just shut up until she was done. Dad beat it out the back door and since all was quiet, Julie shut off the waterworks with a hiccup.

Mom took a deep breath through her nose, blew it out and said, "I think we need to find another way for you to prepare your bottles. I'll clean it up this time and we'll work out a better plan this afternoon. Go on, go feed your baby."

"Sorry, Mom," I winced. "Thanks for your help."

"Uh huh."

That afternoon after school, Mom showed me and Virgil the formula for mixing up the milk using the plastic pitcher we used for lemonade in the summer and the trick to getting the nipples on without spilling the milk in the bottle.

"He's doing pretty good today, I think. Dad says he'll need a lot of TLC to make it though."

"What's that?" asked Virgil.

"What's what?"

"TLC."

"Oh, that means tender loving care, Silly."

"Ha. I thought it was some kind of cow thing. How come he's not in the barn?"

"Dad said it was too big to keep warm enough just for him and you know we can't get that door open anyway." The old garage didn't have a door anymore and Dad had nailed a piece of chicken wire across the opening. He could step right over the wire with his long legs and he'd put a cinder block on each side of the wire so Virgil and I would be able to just climb over it too. "In a couple days, when Ajax gets stronger, Dad said he'd fix a gate we could open and close and make him a halter so we can take him for a walk."

nine

As Bud opened his back door, he growled, "How many times am I going to have to tell you two to go away?"

"Oh, lots and lots. Mom says we have selective hearing. That means we only hear what we want to hear. Besides, we know deep down you really like us and we never see anyone else over here. You'd be so lonely without us. It's not good to be lonely. I think that's why you're grumpy. You're just tired of your own company. We're not just here to visit today though. We came to ask a favor."

"What?"

"Can we use your corral?"

"What for?"

"Ajax needs exercise."

"Ajax?"

"My calf."

"Whose name is Ajax?"

"Yes."

When Bud looked like he was planning to question further regarding the unusual name, Virgil held up a hand to stop him. "It's a whole lot easier if you just go with it. The stuff she does always makes sense to her. She'll explain it, but lots of times it only makes more sense to her and less to you. Just go with it, Man."

"What's wrong with your yard?"

"Ajax might run into something there and get hurt."

Bud just looked at me with his one eyebrow raised, a lot like Mom's, indicating further explanation was needed.

"He's blind."

"You have a blind calf named Ajax?" questioned Bud.

"What's the big deal? Ajax is a fine, strong name for a calf and he needed a new momma. Can we use the corral or not?"

Bud glanced over at the corral with its sagging and broken boards, "It needs some work."

"We can help you fix it," said Virgil.

"I'm sure," said Bud. "Come back Saturday afternoon." He closed the door.

"That Bud still doesn't say much, does he?" I asked.

"Not much," agreed Virgil.

When we returned on Saturday, Bud had a loader tractor with a bucket of fresh hay and a pickup load of new, one by six inch boards. Scowling and using nothing but hand gestures and grunts, Bud directed me to use the pitchfork to toss the hay inside the corral and Virgil to hold up the other end of the boards as he nailed them in place.

Virgil turned on the radio tied to his belt loop and we all worked in time to the beat of the music. After awhile, we paused to rest and I heard the first few notes of one of our favorite songs.

"C'mon, Virg," I hollered as I climbed up to stand in the loader bucket now serving as our stage.

Virgil climbed up as I started to croon, *"They say we're young and we don't know, we won't find out until we grow."*

As Virgil stood up in the bucket, he leaned toward me and sang, *"Well, I don't know if all that's true,"* pointed his thumb at his chest, *"cause you got me and Baby, I got you."*

We both jumped around in a choreographed move to face each other, pointed at each other, and crowed, *"Babe. I got you, Babe. I got you, Babe."*

We turned back to face Bud, our audience. I waved my finger back and forth, then held out my empty hand singing, *"They say our love won't pay the rent, before it's earned our money's all been spent."*

Virgil held both hands palms up and shrugged while he sang, *"I guess that's so, we don't have a pot, but at least I'm sure of all the things we've got."*

We turned to face each other again, *"Babe. I got you, Babe. I got you, Babe."*

Virgil grabbed a handful of hay and held it out to me, then grabbed my hand, *"I got flowers in the spring. I got you to wear my ring."*

I pantomimed tears, smiles, and fear, singing, *"And when I'm sad, you're a clown and if I get scared, you're always around."* I arranged a handful of hay on Virgil's head, *"So let them say your hair's too long, 'cause I don't care, with you I can't go wrong."*

Virgil took my hand and pointed to the horizon, *"Then put your little hand in mine, there ain't no hill or mountain we can't climb."*

"Babe. I got you, Babe. I got you, Babe."

"I got you to hold my hand," sang Virgil.

"I got you to understand," I sang back.

"I got you to walk with me."

"I got you to talk with me."

Virgil kissed my cheek, *"I got you to kiss goodnight."*

I threw my all into the big finish, belting out, *"I got you to hold me tight. I got you, I won't let go. I got you to love me so."*

We held hands and leaned into each other while facing Bud and singing the final "I got you, Babes" then swung our linked hands forward and back, bowing low, just like Sonny and Cher.

Bud leaned against the fence and clapped with just the tiniest hint of a smile curving the corner of his lip.

ten

Just when we thought it was spring, a terrible cold snap hit. April 3, 1975, was so cold it set an all time record at -2 degrees. We had gotten used to playing outside every day without having to cover up everything but our eyeballs and then we were stuck in the house again.

By Sunday afternoon, I was tired of playing in the house with Julie. It was too quiet. I missed Virgil's radio. I went in the kitchen and unplugged Dad's radio he kept on the counter for listening to the market reports in the morning and drug it into the livingroom where Julie was sitting on the floor playing with blocks.

"Let's find some music and dance, Julie," I said as she stared up at me with her toothy grin. I plugged in the radio on the floor by the TV and started slowly turning the tuning dial. "Talking, talking, blah, blah, blah…here we go." I heard *Black Water* by the Doobie Brothers and helped Julie stand up on her wobbly toddler legs. "C'mon, Julie. I'll teach you how to do the Skate," I said as I slid side to side to the music.

Julie laughed and rocked back and forth with her knees locked.

"Now add your arms like this and we'll do the Locomotion. Good job," I said as Julie swung her arms wildly. "Look, Mom, Julie's ready for *American Bandstand* too." Mom had taught me all the 60s dances she knew from high school like the Twist, the Jerk, the Monkey, the Pony, the Swim, the Shimmy, and the Mashed Potato. Most of mine kind of looked the same, but I loved doing them anyway. Mom just smiled and shook her head at us as she walked past with a load of laundry on her hip. The song ended just as Julie fell down on her butt with a plop.

"Ooh, Julie, it's your song," I said as *Lady Marmalade* by LaBelle came on. I had no idea what the lady was singing, but that's what we liked about it. "Hey sister, soul sister, go sister," I sang as I grabbed Julie's hands and pulled her arms back and forth yelling, "Hit it, Julie" when the "Itchy, Gitchy" part came on. We both started just making stuff up, "Itchy, gitchy, ya, ya, hee, hee. Mocho, choca, la, la, vulu. Coocoo, ya, ya, da, da, ma, ma." We kept going even after the song was in English again, until Mom yelled, "Enough already" from the laundry room.

"Hey, Julie, should we play 'Boots'?" I asked.

Julie clapped and cheered, "Yes. Boots."

I ran upstairs to Mom's closet for my gear, came back and put it on, turned off the radio, found the record we needed, and carefully put the needle in place. Julie clapped as I turned to her and the music started playing. *These Boots Were Made for Walkin'* by Nancy Sinatra blared out of the speakers. I was wearing Mom's fashion boots, which were made of some kind of shiny, crinkly, black material and went to Mom's knees, but went all the way to the top of my thighs where I had to hold them up with my hands.

I stomped around the livingroom singing at the top of my lungs, *"These boots were made for walking and that's just what they'll do. One of these days these boots are gonna walk all over you. Start walking boots…"*

When the song was over, Julie laughed and yelled, "Again."

We played it over and over until Mom marched in and turned off the record player with a snap.

"Enough. Julie and I are going to take a nap and you are going outside to play. I think it's warm enough now and you need some fresh air. Why don't you take Ajax for a walk?"

"Yes, Mom." Freedom. I pulled on my coat and boots, ran outside, grabbed Ajax by the halter, and headed toward Bud's house.

I let Ajax in the corral then looked around for Bud. I spotted him leaning against the far side of the barn. He rubbed his face with his hand as I walked toward him.

"Whatchya lookin' at?" I asked as I came to stand next to him.

"Nothing."

Bud's voice sounded funny. He turned his head and did a farmer blow, then sniffed, and wiped his hand on his jeans.

"Got a cold?"

"Nope."

"Whatsamatter?"

"Nothing."

"Huh." We stood in silence for a few seconds.

"Why are we looking at nothing?" I asked.

"Because I'm thinking."

"'Bout what?"

"Nothing."

"Oh." More silence.

"I saw Vietnam on the news last night," I said, shattering the silence.

Bud turned and looked down at me.

"Dad didn't think I was paying attention, but I was. I saw that the Operation Baby Lift plane crashed the other day."

Bud turned his gaze back out to the open prairie and we stood in silence again.

"That's what you're thinking about, isn't it?" I asked quietly.

Bud looked at me again then nodded his head just once. I slipped my hand in his and he squeezed it for just a second as we stood together.

"They're okay, you know," I said.

"How's that?" asked Bud.

"God was with them."

"There is no God in Vietnam," Bud replied.

"Sure there is. God is everywhere."

"Not in a place like Vietnam."

"That's the kind of place where He is the most, where people really need Him."

Bud just stared at me, then out toward the horizon again. I felt I needed to explain myself because Bud needed to understand.

"Have you ever seen *Captain Kangaroo?*" I asked.

Bud remained silent.

"Well, have you?" I asked as I swung the hand he still held so I could get his attention.

"Yes."

I nodded my head at his satisfactory answer and continued.

"Have you seen the part where the Captain looks in on the little people who live behind the books on his bookshelf, but they don't see him?"

Bud didn't say anything, but I could tell he was listening to me.

"I think that's how it works. God is like Captain Kangaroo and we're like the little people who live behind the books on the bookshelf. We just go about our business thinking we live in this great big world and we're all on our own, but really, our little tiny world fits on one of God's bookshelves and He's always watching over us and taking care of us and even moving us around sometimes when we get too close to the edge of the shelf, but we can't see Him."

I caught Bud glancing my way again as I too stared out into space as if looking for the edge of the shelf.

"Orphans means they didn't have moms and dads to take care of them and they needed to find new ones, right?"

Bud cleared his throat and replied, "Right."

"It sounds like there are an awful lot of orphans in Vietnam."

"Yeah."

"Maybe God knew it would be hard to find that many new moms and dads on earth, so he decided it would be faster and easier for Jesus to just pick them up in the clouds and take them to heaven."

Bud squeezed my hand tight as we stood together and looked for God in the endless prairie sky.

eleven

The following Saturday, I rode along with Dad out to Papa and Grandma Cori's to visit while he worked on fixing a tractor to get ready for spring planting.

Grandma was at the kitchen sink washing dishes.

"Did you do the calendar yet, Grandma?" I asked as I walked in and grabbed a handful of pastel colored sugar wafers out of the orange, squeezie-top, Tupperware container on the counter.

"No, not yet."

I got a pen out of the junk drawer, stuck it and my pile of sugar wafers on the counter, then laid my hands flat on the countertop, jumped and pushed up to straighten my arms, banging my toes against the bottom cupboard doors, and twisting around in what I felt was a fine, gymnastic move to land with my butt on the countertop.

"I wish you wouldn't get up there like that. You're going to scuff the cupboards."

"Sorry," I mumbled around a mouthful of sugar. Yes, it was nine o'clock in the morning and I was loading up on sugar. At Papa and Grandma Cori's house, sugar wafers, candy bars, and a variety of ice cream treats from the Schwan's truck delivery man, like orange pushups and strawberry sundae cups, could be had at any time of the day or night, a definite visiting perk. Sugar wafers were a slab of straight sugar frosting made portable by being placed between two thin layers of some edible, Styrofoam-type substance.

I turned and took the calendar down off the wall and, with pen in hand, said, "Ready."

"Low 38, high 61, 0 precipitation. This morning's low was 42. It's going to be a beautiful day looks like, but we could use a little rain."

I neatly wrote the information on the calendar. Every day, Papa or Grandma would write the high and low temperatures from the thermometer mounted on the corner of the kitchen window, the precipitation from the rain gauge on the fence post, and any significant weather events like hail, tornadoes, and blizzards, on the calendar from the bank. The bank calendar always had good sized squares and a pocket for the bill envelopes. Grandma also wrote on the calendar any birthdays, doctor appointments, club meetings like Birthday Club, King's Daughters, Ladies Circle, card club, and events like bowling tournaments, dances, and parties. Papa saved the calendars in a metal filing cabinet in the basement. Every so often, he'd look through them trying to find patterns in the weather or when planning crops or comparing yields as he also wrote down on the calendar how many acres of what crop was planted on which quarter of land on what day and how many acres were harvested yielding how many bushels per acre and sometimes the moisture content of the grain and in which bin it was stored if not taken straight to the elevator.

Grandma Cori's handwriting was light, small, and spidery, which made it hard to read.

I'm left-handed and had learned in school that being left-handed was thought to be hereditary, which meant that someone else in your family had to be left-handed for you to be left-handed. I thought scientists must have gotten that one wrong because I didn't know anyone in my family who was left-handed.

I asked Mom and Dad, "Was I adopted?"

Mom snorted and said, "Definitely not."

"Well then why isn't anybody else in my family left-handed?"

Dad said, "Ask your Grandma Cori."

The next time I saw Grandma, I said, "Hey, Grandma, Dad said to ask you about left-handed people in my family. How come?"

"I'm left-handed."

"No, you aren't. You don't do anything left-handed."

"Well, I was born left-handed."

"Why don't you do things left-handed then?"

"When I was a little girl people thought being left-handed was bad."

"Bad how?"

"Well, not very many people were left-handed and I guess they thought something was wrong with you if you were, so they trained you not to be."

"How'd they do that? I can throw right-handed and use right-handed scissors, but I can't eat or write right-handed at all, no matter how hard I try."

"They forced me to switch hands when I started school."

"But how?"

"Every morning, the teacher used a long rope, wrapped it around and around me and tied my whole left arm to my body, so there was no way I could use it for anything and I couldn't take off the rope all day. I learned to use my right hand right quick or I'd go hungry and wouldn't be able to pass my classes. It was embarrassing too and hard to make friends or play with the other children."

"That's just mean. How could they do that to you?"

"Well, it was better than how your Great Grandma Sadie was treated. People back then thought being left-handed meant she was possessed by evil spirits and it scared them so she got a whipping whenever she got caught using her left hand."

"That's awful. People were really dumb in the olden days."

"I guess they were about some things."

Anyway, that's why Grandma didn't have very good handwriting. It was unnatural for her to write with her right hand, but she always did. She said some things just get drilled in your head and you can't get them out.

After recording the weather information, I started reading the upcoming events Grandma had listed.

"Hey, Grandma Cori, what's a meet try?"

"What?"

"What's a meet try?"

"What are you talking about?"

"Every Saturday in May you have 'meet try', m-e-e-t t-r-y and then somebody's last name like Lenz's or Johnson's or Remily's. What's that?"

"Oh, that says 'nut fry.' Those families all have big nut fries when they work cattle and it's a nice get together."

"But Papa likes his peanuts roasted."

Grandma dropped the pan in the sink. "Well, for goodness sakes, Jennie. It's not that kind of nut."

"Well what kind of nut is it?"

"Haven't you ever heard of a Rocky Mountain Oyster fry?"

"Yeah, but what's that got to do with nuts?"

"Well, that's what Rocky Mountain Oysters are."

"Nuts? They're really big and not very crunchy. I don't like them, but they're kind of tough and chewy like meat, not like peanuts or walnuts."

"They are meat."

"Then why do you call them nuts?"

"Why don't you go out and see how your dad's doing on that tractor?"

I knew that was Grandma-speak for she was done talking about whatever we were talking about. I put the calendar back up on the wall, jumped down from the counter with a sigh, and went to find Dad to ask him my questions.

I found Dad outside the machine shed, near the corral, wiping his hands on a grease rag. Most of the fencing was barbed wire. The corral area and cattle shoot near the barn were all that were made of wood slats and easy to climb. I climbed up the first few boards to lean my elbow against the corner post.

"Hey, Dad?"

"Hey, Jennie?"

"Why does Grandma Cori call a Rocky Mountain Oyster party a nut fry and why did she do that thing where she tells me to come find you because she doesn't want to talk about it anymore?"

"Ah, too many questions make Grandma tired."

"You're a lot younger than Grandma, so you can answer a lot more questions, right, Dad?"

"I guess so," Dad said with a sigh while shaking his head.

"'Cause the only dumb question is the one you don't keep asking until you find an answer, right, Dad?"

"I guess that's right, Jennie. Shoot." When Dad had the time for a long conversation, he didn't just tell me things, he waited for me to come up with the right questions to get the information I was looking for and he asked me questions back so I had to figure out some answers on my own. He said it was good to practice thinking like that so that it would come naturally when no one was around to give you the answers and you needed to solve a problem on your own.

"Why did Grandma Cori call a Rocky Mountain Oyster party a nut fry on the calendar?"

"Because nut fry is a lot shorter and fits on the calendar better."

I sighed dramatically and Dad grinned. He was going to make me work for it.

"Why is a Rocky Mountain Oyster called a nut?"

"Because it is a nut."

"No, it isn't. Grandma said it was meat."

"Nut is a slang word for testicle."

"What's a testicle?"

"A body part."

"A body part on what kind of animal?"

"All kinds."

"It's not a body part on me is it?"

"Nope, just male animals."

"Grandma said people have nut fries when they're working cattle, so is it a cattle part?"

"Yep."

"Why does everybody have them at the same time?"

"Because that's when they have a lot of those parts around."

"How do they get the parts?"

"Well, there are lots of different ways. Some people cut them off or pinch them off, some people burn them off, and some people freeze them off."

"How could they do that and just get one part? Don't you have to butcher cattle to get meat from them because the meat is on the inside?"

"This part is on the outside."

"I don't get it."

"What are the different words we use for cattle?"

"Cows and bulls."

"What else?"

"Ah...heifers and steers. But I don't know which is which there. Cows are moms and bulls are dads, but I don't what heifers and steers are."

"Heifers are girls that aren't moms yet, they haven't had any calves or they're on their first one."

"Okay."

"Steers are boys and where we get the outside parts in question."

"Okay. I still don't get it."

"How do you know just by looking which cattle are girls?" Dad asked.

"Girl cattle have udders where they keep the milk to feed the calves," I replied.

"Right. Look at that bull over there in the pen."

"Uh huh."

"Now look at the cattle in the pasture. What part does the bull have that the others don't have?"

I gasped.

"The missing part is what we're talking about here. Male calves come with that part, but we take it off of some of them so that most of the boys are steers and only a few of the boys are bulls. Just a few really special boys can grow up to be dads."

I stared at Dad in open mouthed astonishment. "You mean you cut them off? You cut them or burn them or freeze them right off their bodies?"

"Yeah."

"Why?"

"Well, because that's the special part that can make calves and turn them into dads or bulls when they grow up."

"Why can't they all be dads?"

"Because they're feeder cattle and you know what that means, right?"

"That when they get big and die they have to get butchered or cut up to make cheeseburgers and meatloaf and roast beef for people to eat and it's okay because that's what God made them for."

"Right. Steers are the best cattle to sell for meat and that's why we raise them, so people castrate calves this time of year."

"What's castrate?"

"That's what you call it when you remove those parts from the male calves to make them steers."

"Wait...so you do it to all the boy calves?"

"Yeah."

"While they're alive and awake?"

"Well, yes."

My voice was getting higher and louder as understanding dawned and I got more and more upset. "So you just hold them down and cut off their private parts, just like that?"

"Pretty much."

"That's awful. How can you do that? You can't go around just hacking off body parts while things are still alive!"

"Don't worry. It doesn't hurt them. They'll be just fine."

"You don't know it doesn't hurt. I bet it does so hurt. How would you feel if someone just decided you'd survive without your parts and they just cut them off?"

"Calm down."

"Heavens to Murgatroid!" I exclaimed as I fully realized what the calendar note meant. "People cut off a bunch of boy calf parts and then they have a party and fry the parts up and eat them while the calves are still right outside crying?"

"It's not quite like that, Jennie."

"It is so. Grandma said it was a nice get together after working cattle. Nice? That is not nice. That is not nice at all."

I gasped again as I had another horrifying thought. "You're going to do that to Ajax too?"

"Yeah, Sweetie, Ajax too."

"Why?" I wailed. "Why can't Ajax grow up to be a daddy bull?"

"Awe, Honey, I told you, only the really special boy calves get to grow up to be bulls."

"Ajax is really special."

"Not that kind of special, Baby Girl. I know he's special to you, but we talked about this when you started taking care of him. He serves a purpose. He has to be sold or butchered eventually just like all the others. It's a business and it's how we make a living, part of how we make money for all the things we need."

"But he could serve a purpose by being a bull, staying here with us, and keeping all his parts."

"No, Jennie. Ajax could never be a bull because there are lots of things wrong with him and he might have calves with those same problems. We don't raise bulls. We raise feeder cattle. Even if we did raise our own bulls, we would only use perfect calves as bulls because we try to make better and better calves so we can make more money when we sell them."

"This is a horrible, awful, terrible way to make money."

"No, it isn't. You like being a farm kid. The calves will be just fine. You'll see."

"Humpf," I scowled, crossed my arms, and stomped across the yard to the pickup.

The next afternoon, Virgil and I met at Bud's corral to exercise Ajax. As soon as I saw Virgil, I demanded, "Do you know what Rocky Mountain Oysters are?"

"Good with ketchup?"

"No, do you know what they really are?"

"Ah…"

"They are parts they cut off of calves while they are still alive."

"Okay…"

"Only boy calves," I said as I stared pointedly below Virgil's waist.

Virgil glanced down. His eyes grew wide, his mouth fell open, and his face paled to a chalky white.

I nodded my head up and down. "Uh huh. They cut them off and then they fry them up and eat them. We are being raised by a bunch of barbarians."

"Wow…"

"They are going to do that to Ajax too. In protest, we are never eating Rocky Mountain Oysters ever again. Not ever." I pointed my finger and poked him in the chest. "Do you hear me, Virgil? I don't care how good you think they taste with ketchup. We will never, ever eat them."

"Yeah, okay," Virgil agreed.

Just then, Bud came out of the shadows by the barn, coughing and leaning over with one hand on his knee. He straightened up and held his hand over his mouth for a long moment, then cleared his throat and said, "Everything okay out here?"

"Everything is fine as long as none of mine and Ajax's friends do something as nasty and horrible as eating Rocky Mountain Oysters," I declared with a scowl I aimed at Bud and Virgil.

Bud looked at me weird. His mouth was screwed up in kind of a half smile, half grimace of pain, but he replied, "Fine by me. They were always a little too chewy for my taste."

twelve

The old barn behind our house wasn't used for anything anymore and Dad didn't really keep it up. The big door was stuck and no matter how much we pushed and tugged, Virgil and I could only get it open enough to squeeze through sideways. At some point in the past, the shutter on the hay loft window blew off and never got fixed. Sitting in the open hay loft window with our feet dangling was our thinking spot.

One morning, I asked Dad to put a hay stack in the hay loft.

"What?" He looked up from the newspaper he was reading at the kitchen table.

"I said, could you please put a load of hay in the hay loft for me?"

"Why?"

"Because it's a hay loft and hay lofts need hay in them."

"Not if there aren't any livestock in the barn to be fed they don't."

"Virgil and I like to sit up there and it would be a lot more comfortable if it had hay in it."

"Hmm. Well, hay is used to feed cattle, so it costs money and your comfort isn't really the biggest consideration."

Mom interjected at this point, "Wait, you kids are playing in the hay loft? I don't think that's safe."

Dad put down the paper and put his hand on the top of my head. Dad's big hand covered the whole top of my head. His thumb and his pinkie touched the tips of my ears and his fingertips on my eyebrows kept my eyes opened wide. He liked to do this when he really wanted me to focus and pay attention to what he was saying.

"You and Virgil know if you screw around someone falls out that window, it's a long way down and you'll break your neck, right?"

"Yes, Dad."

"So you won't ever screw around anywhere near that window, right?"

"Right," I agreed as Dad nodded my head up and down with his hand.

"See there, they know better than to screw around and get hurt," Dad said.

Mom looked like she had another protest working its way up her throat, but Dad said, "They'll be fine, Sweet Cheeks." Mom's protest died in her mouth as she smiled and turned back to the dishes.

Dad winked at me and I smiled back at him. We both knew him calling Mom 'Sweet Cheeks' worked every time to knock her train right off the tracks.

The next afternoon after school, there wasn't an expensive load of hay in the barn, but there were half a dozen straw bales arranged like bench seats near the window. Straw's not near as comfy as hay, but a whole lot better than bare wood.

I ran back down the stairs and across the street to Virgil's bedroom window, tossed a handful of gravel at it, and sang, "Sha, la, la, la, la, la, la, la, la, la, la, da, la, tee, da, sha, la, tee, da," from the chorus of our song, *Brown Eyed Girl* by Van Morrison. That was the signal to meet in the hay loft as soon as we could get away. *Brown Eyed Girl* was our song because it sounded just like us, laughing and running, skipping and jumping, all with a transistor radio.

I was snuggled down on our new straw couch, deep into *Misty of Chincoteague* by Marguerite Henry by the time Virgil was able to get away.

"Check out the new furniture. Cool," Virgil said as he sat in his new straw chair and bounced up and down a little. "Where're we at today, Squirt?"

I always loved books, even before I could read them. Dad told me if I opened a book, I could explore every place ever, all of this world and all of the make-believe worlds ever dreamed up, this time, past time, and future time, every place ever, and still be home in time for supper.

I couldn't wait to get started, but he said I had to go to school to learn how to read before I could go anywhere else.

I went to school figuring we'd have to gear up to it a little, but surely by the third or fourth day I would be able to read. Weeks passed and still nothing. I loved my kindergarten teacher, she was as nice as she could be, but she was not telling me what I needed to know.

After months of waiting, I finally demanded an explanation and was told that I would learn to read the next year in first grade. Next year? That wasn't the story I had gotten at all. What was wrong with these people?

By the time Mrs. Holmquist and Mr. Soundy finally got around to teaching me to read, I was in a hurry. I had a lot of reading and thereby exploring to do. I read all of the time, whenever I could.

Virgil didn't like to read, but he did like to go places, so I read the books and then told him about the faraway places I found in them.

"We're in Chincoteague today. It's an island in the Atlantic Ocean off the coast of Virginia. Wild ponies live there and every year people go out to the island and try to catch some of the ponies and swim them back to the mainland to tame them and keep them to ride and as pets. It sounds like a pretty place, a little like here on the prairie only with water and sand instead of grass and fields."

"Cool. Did it make the list?"

"I think so. I'd like to see dozens of wild ponies running on the beach with their manes and tails blowing in the wind and the waves trying to catch them." I kept a list of real places I read about that I wanted to go see in person someday. Every once in awhile I would rate my list, putting a number one next to the place I wanted to see the most, a two by the next, and so on. It was hard to decide though and whenever I finished a book, the place I had just read about was usually the place I wanted to see most, so my list had a lot of scribbled out numbers on it.

We rearranged our new bales a few times until they were just right and Virgil cut the twine on one of them with his pocket knife so we could pile up the straw like a bean bag chair. Our thinking spot was now quite comfy.

thirteen

Spring on the Great Plains is a time of hope and infinite possibility. After the long, often brutal winter, it's a time to start again.

Outsiders, people in the cities who don't know sodbusters and understand their way of life, may think them boring, plodding, and unadventurous, being so tied to the land. People who think that would be wrong. Farmers are, by necessity, some of the world's greatest dreamers and risk takers. Every spring they roll the dice and go all in, betting every penny they can get their hands on and even their very lives, that this will be the year, the year that everything will go as planned and the plan will be a good one. This will be the year that God, The Weather, and fate will all work in their favor and the harvest will be plentiful. This will be the year they are not plagued by floods, droughts, hail, tornadoes, fire, and pestilence during the growing season and when they make it to harvest, the market for the crops they chose will work in their favor.

So many disastrous things, completely out of their control, could happen, yet they bet it all every spring. There could be no gamble more unpredictable and fraught with risk. Only true dreamers would keep on believing, no matter how many times their hopes have been crushed in the past, that something wonderful is still possible with the coming of a new spring.

Young or old, farmer or no, living in a farming community, it was impossible not to be filled with the excitement and anticipation of spring when it finally arrived. Tractors, plows, and drills were brought out of machine sheds and barns, washed off, shined up, greased down, and checked over to ensure that everything was in working condition and ready to start spring planting.

With ancient machinery that had had little to no maintenance for several years, Bud had a lot to do before getting out in the field. Virgil and I were on hand to help out and keep him company.

"Did you know that dogs have a third eyelid to protect their eyeball from irritants and they can't see the colors red or green?"

"Up to 'D' in Grandma's encyclopedias I take it?" asked Bud.

"Yep."

"You're moving right along through those things."

"Well, I'm just skimming some now. That means looking at books really fast and not reading all the words, just some of them, and only slowing down to read all the words when something looks good. They use a lot of really big words in the World Book Encyclopedias. Some words aren't even in English. And they write about some really boring stuff. I tried to read it all, but it's just too hard and takes too long. Now I'm only reading the good stuff."

"How do you suppose they know dogs can't see red or green?" I mused. "They can't ask them what they can see and what they can't, so how do they know? I mean you can't ask a dog to fetch a blue ball, but don't fetch a red ball, right? Is a dog's red and green the same as a person's red and green? Nobody could really know what anybody sees, could they? I bet one person's red and green isn't even the same as another person's red and green. Like maybe I call the sky

blue and the grass green and so does Virgil, but what if the
blue color I see is actually the purple color Virgil sees and
the green color Virgil sees is actually the orange color I see,
but we both call what we see blue and green so we don't
know one person's blue is purple and another person's green
is orange because we can't see from inside the other person's
head to see if it's really the same thing. And dogs can't talk
to humans about it at all.

Bud and Virgil just stared at me, then at each other.

Virgil responded to Bud's unspoken question by saying,
"Yeah, sometimes it makes you tired to follow her around in
her head, but you don't have to say anything unless she takes
a breath and looks at right at you. Even then, if you're not
sure what she's talking about anymore, just nod your head
and say, 'Hmmm' and she'll keep going 'til she runs out of
steam."

I scowled at Virgil as I wasn't sure I liked the idea that
he didn't really pay attention to me, but then I got distracted
by another thought in my head and followed it like I would a
butterfly going past, which made me forget about being mad.

"Read us an Encyclopedia Brown mystery," Virgil said
as he settled down on the ground next to Bud's open tool
box, ready to hand Bud wrenches and sockets and the like as
needed, while he tried to get the tractor running. Virgil was
an experienced tool hander having helped his dad and his
dad's pit crew of misfit teenage boys, work on stock cars.

"Okay. *The Case of the Mysterious Tramp......How did John
Morgan give himself away?*"

Before Bud and I could even open our mouths to
speak, Virgil said, "Duh. If he really was in the truck while
Clancy was checking the radiator, all he would see would be
the hood. That one was too easy."

"Dang it. You always beat me to the solution, even on
stuff I know about. The only one I beat you on was *The Case
of the Secret Pitch.*"

"She beat you on a baseball mystery?" Bud asked Virgil.

"Hey, I play baseball too, you know," I interjected.

"The solution wasn't about baseball," Virgil explained. "It was about the date on a letter. I didn't remember that June only had 30 days and she did."

"I could've beat you even if it was about baseball."

"Sure, Squirt."

"I bet you don't know that the first officially recorded baseball game in U.S. history happened in 1846 in Hoboken, New Jersey when the New York Nine beat the New York Knickerbockers 23-1 in four innings. I know that because I get my information from places like the World Book Encyclopedia, not from baseball cards that double as chewing gum wrappers."

Virgil turned to Bud again and said, "Yeah, sometimes the Smarty Pants thing is *really* annoying, but she always feels bad later and does something nice to make up for it if she says it all snotty like that."

"Why do you keep telling him stuff about me like I'm not standing right here?" I asked Virgil.

"It's a guy thing. Dad told the pit crew guys have to stick together and, what did he say? Pool something. Oh, yeah, 'pool resources in order to understand women'. That means they should tell the other guys whatever stuff they find out about girls so they can all get smarter faster and they won't all do the same dumb stuff."

"Ugh," I huffed in disgust.

Bud just shook his head at us.

I got lost in my own thoughts for awhile as Bud and Virgil continued to tinker with the tractor. All of a sudden, I yelled, "SUPERCALIFRAGILISTICEXPIALIDOCIOUS!" making Bud drop his tool, hit his head on the engine block, and growl, "What the hell was that?" as he crawled out from under the tractor.

"Oh, sorry," I replied. "Did you see *The Wonderful World of Disney* last Sunday? The movie was called *Mary Poppins*. It was about a magical nanny in London, England. A nanny is a full time babysitter. She sang this song about being smart and in the song it said that if you say

SUPERCALIFRAGILISTICEXPIALIDOCIOUS loud enough, you'll always sound precocious."

Bud just raised his one eyebrow at me kind of mean-like.

"Yeah, Dad told me to knock it off. He said in my case it was overkill. I'm not sure what he meant by that."

Bud made a sudden, loud noise.

"Did you just snort?" I asked.

Bud didn't respond, he simply crawled back under the tractor.

Some time later, Bud tossed a wrench down on the ground and hit the side of the tractor with his hand.

"Whatsamatter?" I asked.

"It's not working," Bud replied.

"You know, I think it's because you're not talking to it," I said.

"Yeah, have you named her?" said Virgil.

"Her?" asked Bud.

"The tractor. You need to name her like the guys name the cars and then talk to her like a girl you're trying to figure out," Virgil said.

"Dad's 806 with the cab doesn't have a name really, but he calls it 'Old Girl' and pats its tires when he gets it to run again. I think you talk to it like a girl when you're trying to talk it into running right, but it's not quite there yet or when it does a good job. If it's not doing anything at all, you need to cuss it," I said.

"Oh yeah, Man. You definitely need to use more cuss words if it's not doing anything," Virgil agreed.

"Cuss it, huh?" asked Bud.

"Yeah, yell things like, 'you stinking piece of…'," I interjected.

Bud held up a hand to stop me, "I got it."

"There are all kinds of cuss words you can use," said Virgil.

"We won't tell you said them in front of us and we're smart enough not use them ourselves in front of adults," I assured him.

"I already know all the cuss words there are," boasted Virgil. "I even know some I haven't told Jennie."

"You do?" I questioned. "Why didn't you tell me? I tell you everything I know."

"Dad said some of the stuff I've heard in the garage I can't ever repeat so Mom can never get wind of it. If Mom found out I knew a few of those words or that I told Jennie about them, Dad said she would have a fit so bad it would make the wrath of God seem like afternoon recess in kindergarten."

"I can't believe you don't tell me. I can keep a secret, you know."

"Dad said it's not right. Even if you're a girl who doesn't always seem like a girl."

"Fine then."

"Don't go and pout like a girl. I just can't tell, okay?"

Bud cleared his throat, "Just hand me that electrical tape."

Even though he didn't cuss at it in front of us, Bud did eventually get the old tractor running again and it looked like he might actually put in some acres.

fourteen

"Jennie-bean!" hollered Dad as he stopped the pickup in the driveway and climbed out. "I've got a surprise."

"What is it?" I asked, as I abandoned lining up my marbles in the sidewalk crack and ran towards him.

"Let's go inside so Julie can see too," Dad said as I ran along beside him and grabbed his hand.

"Julie," I yelled as we entered the kitchen, "Dad has a surprise for us. C'mere. Hurry up."

Julie toddled through the doorway, sucking her middle two fingers and scratching her nose with her pointer finger.

"Now can we see, Dad?" I begged, tugging on his arm.

Dad squatted down next to Julie and said, "I think I need some hugs and kisses first." I plopped down on one of his knees, threw my arms around his neck, and started kissing all over his face while Julie leaned against his other knee and grinned around the fingers in her mouth.

Startled, I leaned back as far as my arms would let me as Dad's shirt moved.

"Watch it there. You're squishing the surprise," said Dad.

"What is it?" I asked again.

"Look inside my shirt pocket and see, but move real slow."

I leaned back in, pulled back the edge of his pocket with my fingertip, and just barely stuck my nose over the opening to look down. Nestled inside Dad's pocket were two little brown balls of fur. I stuck my nose almost inside his pocket to get a closer look when the fur ball jumped and I fell to the floor on my bottom in surprise.

Dad caught the ball in mid-air and held it out to me. Julie squealed, "Kitty!"

"No, it's not a kitty, Punkin'. It's a baby bunny," Dad said.

I cupped the tiny ball in both of my hands and Dad reached back in his pocket to get the other bunny for Julie to hold. Julie reached out and grabbed the tiny bunny's neck in a stranglehold.

"Easy," warned Dad, as he saved the bunny from Julie's clutches by prying back her grubby, little fingers one by one.

"Just pet the bunny, Julie, real careful-like. See," Dad demonstrated, stroking one finger down the bunny's back.

Julie touched one fingertip to the top of the bunny's head then pulled her hand behind her back, looking at Dad for approval.

"That's right," he praised. "You sit down and I'll put the bunny in your lap, okay?"

Julie plopped down with her legs sticking straight out and Dad gently placed the bunny in the middle of her thighs.

Julie patted it a few times, but then it started to crawl up her body, trying to get away, which scared her. She reached her arms out to Dad, screaming and crying.

Dad scooped up the bunny in one hand and Julie in the other hand to hold them both against his chest. "It's okay. See, everybody's fine," Dad crooned as he rubbed his cheek against Julie's head and his thumb against the bunny's head.

I ignored the commotion Julie was making and stared intently at my bunny as I held it in my hands. I drew up my knees, placing my elbows on them, and bringing my cupped hands right up close to my face so that the bunny and I were looking each other straight in the eye.

The bunny was so scared. His heart was thumping against my hand like it was going to pop right out of his body and beating so fast I couldn't count the beats. I looked in his eyes and it was like he looked right through me and couldn't see me at all. His eyes started darting in all directions. I had to do something to calm him down.

I brought my legs down to cross them Indian style and held my left arm across my body like I was holding a baby doll. The bunny burrowed his head down in the crook of my elbow. I held my arm close to my body, let him squish his head down under my arm to hide his face, and laid my hand on his back so he was all covered up. I think he thought if he couldn't see anything, nothing could see him, he was invisible.

Julie started to quiet down and as the room got quiet and I held real still, the bunny's heartbeat started to slow down and not thump quite so hard.

"Where did you get them, Dad?" I whispered.

"I caught them coming out of their nest when I was tilling," Dad whispered back.

I felt the bunny's frantic heartbeat and thought about how scared he was.

"We have to put them back, Dad," I declared.

"We can't, Jennie-bean."

"Why not?"

"Their nest is gone. That's why I caught them. I was about to run over their nest with the plow. I was trying to save them."

"Oh. Well, I don't think we can keep them. They're really, really scared."

"No, you're right, you can't keep them. They're not like Peter was, they're wild and they're jackrabbits. They need to be able to run. I just thought you girls would like to see them and play with them a little before we let them go." Peter was a white rabbit I got one year for Easter and kept in a cage in the yard. He was domesticated, which Grandpa said meant he was born in a cage and didn't know there was any other way to live, so he didn't mind it. Peter never really did anything but sit in the cage and sleep and eat lettuce and carrots. Virgil's brother, Edward, used to poke a stick at him through the wire of the cage. Peter pretended not to care, but one day when Edward stood close with his back to the cage, Peter saw his chance, stuck his mouth through the hole, and bit Edward on the elbow. I'd never seen Peter move that much before. Edward cried like a baby, but he stayed away from Peter's cage after that.

"What did their nest look like before you plowed it up?" I asked as I continued to stroke the tiny bunny hiding under my arm.

"It's kind of a hole under the grass and stubble that their momma lines with her fur."

I considered that for a few minutes. "We can't just let them go. They won't know what to do. We need to make them a safe place to hide. Mrs. Carlson's big tom cat, Scratch, will catch them and eat them if they don't have anywhere to hide."

"Okay. We'll work something up for them. Why don't you see if Mom has a shoebox we can put them in for now?"

Mom found us a shoebox and helped us poke holes in the top before placing the bunnies inside and tying the box closed with a piece of yarn.

"Mom, we need some fur. Do we have some fur?"

"Ah, not that I can think of, no."

"Huh." I sat and thought about the problem for a minute. "Wait, yes, we do."

"We do?" asked Mom.

"Yes. Will you take me to Grandma Mae's house quick to get it?"

"I guess, but what are you talking about?"

"My stove."

"Your stove?" Mom questioned, still not understanding the connection.

"Yes. My mink stove. That's made of fur, isn't it?"

"Oh, your mink *stole* at Grandma's house," Mom confirmed.

"That's what I said, my mink stove."

"Uh huh. Well, whichever, that's not real fur, Jennie. Besides, if you cut it up for bunny houses, you couldn't play dress up with it anymore. I think your bunnies just need something soft and warm to snuggle up in. Fur is all the momma bunny had available for that. Why don't we cut up some old diapers for them? They've been washed lots and lots of times, so they're really soft and snuggly. That'll do."

"I guess it will have to," I sighed dramatically.

I wanted to make the bunnies a nest on the edge of Mom's garden spot so Dad would be sure not to get them with the plow or the drill or any other implement, but Mom said that was a might too generous and we settled on the far inside corner of the field behind the house. It was on the edge of the dirt, so it was easy to dig, but next to a big rock so Dad wouldn't hit it. I was satisfied we'd done the best we could for them.

fifteen

On April 30, 1975, the news said Saigon fell. I wasn't sure what that meant. How could a place fall?

I watched the six o'clock news all the way through, trying to figure out what they were talking about. I wasn't sure the people talking on TV knew what it meant either.

The pictures looked really scary and confusing. People were running everywhere, screaming and crying, pushing and shoving, trying to get into helicopters. You could see fire and smoke in the distance. There were soldiers who looked dirty, tired, and upset, trying to help the people, but looking every which way like someone was going to sneak up and get them if they didn't hurry.

I thought 'Saigon fell' might mean that the war was over and all the soldiers could come home, but no one said that. There had been soldiers in Vietnam for as long as I could remember things. I couldn't be certain, but I thought there had been soldiers in Vietnam since before I was born, so it would really be something if this meant everyone could come home after such a long time.

I mulled it over for awhile then decided to go ask Bud about it. It had been raining most of the day, so I knew he couldn't be out in the field and was probably in the machine shed working on something.

105

I stopped across the street at Virgil's and knocked on the door. Virgil's sister Roberta flung open the door as she ran by on her way up the stairs and yelled, "Jennie's here!"

Virgil came out of the kitchen with a milk mustache and two cookies in his hand.

"Hey, Squirt. Want some?" he offered.

"Naw, I'm good. I'm going over to ask Bud a question. Wanna come?"

"Sure," he said with a shrug as he reached for his jacket on the hook by the door.

"Virgil! Do not leave this house without your golashes on. I don't want mud tracked to the four corners," ordered his mom from the kitchen.

"I don't know where they are," Virgil hollered back.

"Then you'd better find them or you're not going anywhere, Mister," she responded.

Virgil sighed and rolled his eyes. "I'll catch up."

"Okay."

I ran ahead to Bud's to try to beat the rain that started pouring down just before I reached the open machine shed doors.

The pounding rain on the old roof's tin patches caused a horrible racket that echoed through the nearly empty building.

Bud was on his knees next to the drill, with his back to the door, facing the dark, windowless area of the shed.

Still deep in thought myself, I approached him soundlessly on the soft, dirt floor. When I reached out and touched his shoulder, his good hand flew up across his chest, snatched hold of my wrist, and flipped me down on my back in the dirt with a quiet thud that knocked the air out of my lungs.

He leaned his big body over me with is hard, muscle roped forearm across my throat, crushing my windpipe. I tried to move my head, but that only made him push harder. I tried to yell, but only the tiniest squeak made it past his arm. I tugged at him with my hands, but his arm was like a tree trunk and didn't budge a bit. I kicked my legs, but couldn't move my upper body at all, trapped as it was beneath his rock solid arm.

My legs were getting heavy and hard to lift. I couldn't breathe and nothing I did changed that. It was getting hard to hear. Everything seemed muffled and far, far away, except for the drum of my heartbeat pounding in my head. My chest hurt without air to fill my lungs.

What I could see started to get black around the edges and the light was a circle that kept getting smaller and smaller, just like the screen on Great Grandma Sophie's old, black and white TV when you turned it off. It didn't shut off right away, the circle of light on the screen got smaller and smaller, until it was just one little dot that blinked, then the screen turned black, and the TV was off. That's how I felt, like any second, my light and my life would blink out and I would be forever turned off.

My light was almost a dot in the middle when suddenly, the pressure released and I gasped for air. Still gulping in as much air as I could, I unconsciously rolled over and curled up in a ball to try to protect myself from further harm.

Slowly, my light got big again so that I could see and I started hearing noises besides my heartbeat drum. What I heard was Virgil screaming, "You're hurting her! You're hurting Jennie! Stop it! Get away from her, you big, ugly brute! I'm gonna kill you! Don't you touch her!"

I rolled over to see Virgil hanging on Bud's back with his arm around Bud's neck, pulling his hair, kicking his sides and stomach, all red in the face from screaming. Bud was twisting side to side, trying to get Virgil, the crazy, biting monkey, off his back, but with only one arm that could reach behind him, it was proving impossible.

I started to call to Virgil to stop, but nothing came out. I swallowed hard and tried again, but it was still only a croak. I coughed and rubbed my throat, then crawled over to them and tried to grab Virgil's flailing foot, still croaking for him to stop. Blessedly, my croaks got loud enough for him to hear me and he jumped off Bud's back.

It was a three way standoff with all of us on our knees, panting for air, and looking from one to the other in wide eyed shock.

Long moments later, Virgil jumped up and reached for my hand.

"C'mon, Jennie. Let's get out of here. Can you get up? Are you okay?"

I grabbed Virgil's hand and stood with my knees shaking.

"Are you okay, Squirt? Answer me," he demanded.

I touched my throat and nodded my head.

Satisfied with my answer, Virgil turned to Bud and yelled, "You hurt her, you crazy freak! You're five times as big as she is. You could have killed her like breaking a twig. You stay away from us. I wish you'd never found the road home. Go get lost again."

Virgil headed for the door, pulling me along behind him, yelling, "We are never coming back here!"

Bud responded with an angry, "Good. I never wanted you damn brats here in the first place. Good riddance."

As Virgil drug me down the driveway, I looked back to see Bud framed in the doorway. The drops running down his cheek didn't look like rain to me.

Virgil was breathing heavy and working his lip with his teeth as he stomped along toward our barn, but he didn't say anything.

When we got to the loft, he gently pushed me down to sit on the straw bales, then stood with his hands on his hips and asked, "What happened back there?"

"I'm not sure," I croaked, then cleared my throat and tried again. "I think I startled him."

"So he decided to choke the life out of you? That's messed up. You need to tell your mom. Your dad will go over there and clean his clock but good."

"No."

"What do you mean, 'no'?"

"Don't tell," I commanded.

"We have to tell. You're hurt."

"I'm okay."

"No, you're not. Some crazy idiot just about strangled you."

"I'm okay and we are not going to tell. I don't want Bud to get in trouble."

"Who gives a crap about Bud?"

"I do. He's my friend and yours too."

"Some friend."

"It's my secret. I get to decide and I say we are not going to tell. Pinkie promise me."

"Fine," Virgil sighed. "What about the bruises on your neck?"

I touched my throat lightly and asked, "Can you see some?"

"Yes. The whole thing is blue already. He really did a number on you."

"We'll just say I got them playing Red Rover. You know I'm so short I get clotheslined all the time playing that game. We will not tell anyone, ever. Got it?"

"Okay, but I'm not happy about it."

"You don't have to be happy, you just have to keep your trap shut."

We sat in silence for a few minutes, then I said quietly, "Thank you for saving me, Virgil."

"Always and forever," he replied as we sat and looked out the loft window at the now softly falling rain.

sixteen

I liked school, but the last month always took a long, long time and it was very hard to pay attention knowing that summer was right around the corner.

Somehow, the teacher's whistle got so quiet in the spring sunshine at afternoon recess that you couldn't hear it at all when she blew it to signal time to go back inside.

I daydreamed a lot on a good day, but being preoccupied with thoughts of Bud and trying to sort out what had happened, I spaced off much more than usual.

My teacher snapped her fingers in front of my nose, saying, "Earth to Jennie. Jennie, come in, please." The whole class laughed and looked my way, making me blush bright red. "Hello? Where were you?"

"Uh, I guess my mind was someplace else," I replied in embarrassment.

"Well, it needs to be here and focused on your schoolwork. It's not summer yet. Pay attention," she ordered as she tapped the paper on my desk.

I tried, but it was a struggle.

Saturday, Virgil and I were in the back yard with one end of a piece of rope tied to the clothesline post. Virgil was swinging the other end in circles as I stood in the middle, studying the rope as it swung round and round.

Mom came out the back door with a basket on her arm. "Why don't you kids come help me plant the garden?" she called. "I should have done it this morning, but I wanted to wait until Julie was down for her nap so she didn't get in the middle of things to help."

"Well, I guess it's less girly than trying to help Grace here figure out how to jump rope without getting smacked in the head or falling on her face," answered Virgil.

"I'm getting better," I groused.

"Uh huh," Virgil said in a disbelieving tone.

"I think you will both enjoy it and maybe if you put a little work into it, you'll want to watch it grow and won't be so quick to gobble it all up without sharing. Huh, Sweet Pea?" Mom said as she swatted me on the behind when I walked by.

Mom and Dad called me Sweet Pea because back when we were real little and didn't know better, Virgil and I started on opposite ends of the row and met in the middle, eating our way through all of Mom's sweet peas before she could pick them. We were so full, we just laid down right there in the middle of the garden and took a nap in the sunshine. Dad said we were curled up like two peas in a pod...stuffed with peas in a pod. Mom was so upset she was crying by the time she found us.

Mom sent us off to find sticks to use as stakes, then laid packages of seeds out in a row. She made the rows straight by putting sticks on each end and tying a string between them. She measured our hands, fingers, arms, and feet with a yard stick and told us which body part to use to measure the distance between seeds and which knuckle to use to measure how deep, depending on the directions on the package. When we finished planting a row, Mom poked the empty package down on the stick so she could tell what was what before the plants got big.

Virgil's radio was playing while we worked in the dirt.

"Ooh, Virgil, turn it up," I said. *Sunshine on My Shoulders* by John Denver was playing:

Sunshine on my shoulders makes me happy. Sunshine in my eyes can make me cry. Sunshine on the water looks so lovely. Sunshine almost always makes me high. If I had a day that I could give to you, I'd give to you a day just like today. If I had a song that I could sing for you, I'd sing a song to make you feel this way. If I had a tale that I could tell you, I'd tell a tale sure to make you smile. If I had a wish that I could wish for you, I'd make a wish for sunshine all the while.

Mom and I sang along, me on the melody, Mom on the harmony.

"Isn't that just the prettiest song?" I asked. "It makes me feel all warm inside."

"I like that one too," Mom agreed. "There. I believe we're done. Thank you for your help. I couldn't have done it before Julie woke up without you. You did a fine job."

Virgil nodded his acknowledgement and wiped his dirty hands on the legs of his jeans. "I'm parched."

Mom said, "Get a drink from the spigot and screw on that hose and drag it over here, if you can, please."

Virgil went off to do as she asked and I wandered over to the barn, chewing on the sweet part at the bottom of a blade of grass, thinking as I went.

When Virgil caught up with me in the loft, I announced, "He didn't mean it."

"Who didn't mean what?" asked Virgil.

"Bud. He didn't mean it."

"Well, mean it or not, he hurt you and he might do worse next time."

"It was an accident. He was lost in a daymare."

"What's a daymare?"

"It's when you have a daydream with your eyes open, only it's scary like a nightmare when you're asleep. He was lost in a daymare and he couldn't see me."

"What do you mean he couldn't see you? You were right in front of him as he was squishing you like a bug."

"He couldn't see me though. I looked in his eyes and I could tell he couldn't see me because he was seeing scary stuff in his head instead."

"I don't know," grumbled Virgil.

"It's true. His eyes looked just like that bunny Dad caught for us a couple of weeks ago. His eyes were really, super scared like the bunny's, looking at me, but seeing right through me because he was so, so scared."

"Maybe, but he's still dangerous. I don't want you to go over there."

"He needs us. He didn't mean to hurt me. He won't do it again. I just have to remember not to sneak up on him and scare him like I did that day."

"I don't like it."

"C'mon, Virgil. It'll be okay. He's big and could have snapped me like a twig, just like you said, but he didn't. He was lost in the daymare and didn't recognize me, but deep down, he knew not to really hurt me. We have to forgive him."

"I don't know."

"Please, Virgil?" I pleaded in a voice close to tears. "Bud needs us to help him find the road home from that dark, scary place in his head so he can feel the sunshine again."

"Fine, Squirt," Virgil agreed with a sigh, "If it will make you happy."

"Thank you," I whispered as I gazed across the field toward Bud's place. "He just needs us to be his friends and love him back home."

seventeen

I tried and tried to talk to Bud, but either he wasn't home or he wouldn't answer the door, no matter how long I knocked.

I decided I had to catch him outside where it was harder for him to hide from me. I asked Virgil to borrow his Dad's binoculars again for further surveillance, hid in our lilac bush fort, and watched Bud's yard every afternoon, but never caught sight of him. I was getting frustrated.

"How am I going to catch Bud to tell him I want us to be friends again?"

"Maybe you need some bait," said Virgil.

"Bait?" I asked.

"Yeah. If you're going to catch fish, you have to have bait on your hook, something fish like to eat, like corn or crickets or worms."

"That's a great idea, Virgil. I can do that."

"Want me to dig up some night crawlers for you?"

"Very funny, Wise Acre."

The next day as I was leaving the house, I said, "I need to go to Grandma Mae's after school, but could you please come pick me up about supper time?"

"What for?" Mom asked.

"I need Grandma's help with something. Do I have to explain?"

"I guess not, but go straight to Grandma's and don't dawdle. I'll tell her you're coming."

"Thanks."

As I burst through Grandpa and Grandma's back door, I announced, "Hey, Grandma, I got some sugar for you."

"Oh, good, Jennie-bird. I need a little right here," Grandma replied as she tapped her cheek.

I kissed the spot and gave her a big hug.

"I need your help, Grandma."

"Okay. What can I do for you?"

"I need to make a big batch of molasses cookies, with plenty of extras, to give to a friend who needs them real bad."

"We can do that. Check and see if we have enough molasses. I think we were getting low last time and Grandpa and I haven't made it to town in awhile, so it's still on the list."

I held the bottle up to the light, "Does it look like enough?"

"Just right for one special batch."

Grandma got the cookie mixing bowl down from the shelf and we gathered up the ingredients from around the kitchen.

As the last pan came out of the oven, Grandma noticed I hadn't said anything in awhile and I was looking sad with my lip sticking out in a pout.

"You'd better smile or a birdie's going to poop on that lip."

"I have a worry, Grandma."

"Goodness. Let's see if we can rock it away," Grandma said as she took my hand and walked to the green brocade chair by the window.

Even though I was much too big a girl, I snuggled up on Grandma's lap, sure to sit high enough that when she tilted her head, her cheek would lie against my forehead. Grandma's cheek was soft, round, and a little bit fuzzy, so it felt just like a ripe peach. Grandma was soft and sweet all over and smelled like talcum powder and sunshine. When she held you, it felt like you were all covered up in a featherdown pillow, safe and peaceful.

After we'd rocked quietly for a few minutes, Grandma asked, "What seems to be the trouble, Chickadee?"

"How many soldiers died in Vietnam?" I asked.

Grandma's foot stopped the chair from rocking, she sat up straighter, and held my face in her hands to look me in the eye, "Why would you ask such a thing?"

"My friend Bud was a soldier and he's real sad most all the time and sometimes he's scared and angry, so I was wondering if maybe some of his friends died."

Grandma leaned back in the chair, held my face to her chest with her hand, and resumed rocking, though much faster than before.

"Little girls shouldn't be wondering about such things," Grandma declared.

"I can't help what I wonder about. How many, Grandma?"

"Oh, gracious, thousands and thousands, Sweet Girl, almost too many to count. Such an awful shame, but not something little girls should think about. Hush now. Close your eyes and let's rock the troubles away," Grandma said as she kissed my forehead. "Hush now."

When I got home, I carefully wrapped a plate piled high with molasses cookies in tin foil, Scotch taped a note to the top, and left it on Bud's back step so he couldn't miss it going in or out. The note said, *"I forgive you. It was an accident. Can we be friends again? Check one: □ yes □ no Jennie"*

eighteen

Bud didn't return my note with an answer checked, but I decided to take not answering at all as a maybe. I was more confident in the maybe when I started seeing him outside in the yard again.

The Saturday morning before Memorial Day, I decided it was time to catch him.

"It's too late to go inside, Bud Nagle. I've already seen you," I started hollering while I was still a ways down the road from Bud's yard, "You might just as well give up and talk to me. I've already explained how Grandma calls me tenacious. Grandpa says that means stubborn as a mule and twice as ornery. It'll be a whole lot less trouble for both of us if you just give in now and don't make me get out the big guns. I'm not sure what those are yet, but don't you worry, I'll think of something. I'm real good at thinking up stuff, 'specially annoying stuff. Mom says I'm a master at it. I can aggravate the snot out of you if I put my mind to it. Yes, siree, Bob."

Bud drew in a deep breath for a big sigh as he turned from the fence to face me. "I thought you said you weren't coming around here anymore."

"I didn't say that. Virgil did. He didn't mean it either. He was just upset."

"Well, whoever said it, it was a damn fine idea."

"No, it wasn't."

"Yeah, it was."

"No, you need us. We're your friends. Everybody needs friends and you haven't got any others around that I've seen."

"Look, Kid, you don't need me in your life. Virgil was right. I could've hurt you."

"You didn't mean to."

"It doesn't matter. He's right. I'm a crazy freak and you need to stay away from me."

"He didn't mean that and it's not true."

"Yes, Kid, it is. A lot of people have gotten hurt around me and I need to be left alone."

"It's not your fault. You wouldn't hurt anybody on purpose."

"You don't know that."

"Yes, I do. I know stuff about people. I study things and Papa says I've got a good gut. I've studied you and my gut says you're a good guy, even if you don't think so."

"Now who's the crazy one? I almost killed you."

"But it was all because I snuck up on you when you were stuck in a daymare. I'll just be sure to warn you I'm coming from now on." Bud scowled at me in silence. I put my hands on my hips and scowled right back at him. "I'm not giving up. You're gonna blink first."

We continued to stare at each other for some time. I screwed my mouth up to blow at the fly that landed on my cheek, but held my fierce eye scowl. Bud blinked.

He slapped the fence post with his hand and turned to face the pasture beyond the house. "It's called a flashback. Daymare's not even a word," Bud muttered.

"Whatever it is is scary, huh?" I asked as I too turned to look out at the oceans of grass waving in the breeze and reached for his hand. He didn't say anything, but he didn't pull his hand away either.

"You know, when I have a bad dream, telling Mom about it helps it go away and be not so scary in my head.

Flashbacks seem a lot like bad dreams. Maybe telling me about it would help it go away."

"Can't," replied Bud.

"Why not?"

"I can't tell a little girl about something like that."

"Great Grandma Sophie says I have an 'old soul.' That means I understand stuff you'd think I would be too young to get. I won't tell anyone. I'm good at listening if I want to be."

"It'd been on my mind because of the news. It rained a lot in Vietnam and the rain on the tin sounded a lot like gunfire. I guess that's what started it."

I nodded in understanding, but Bud didn't say anything more.

After awhile I asked, "Can you tell when one is coming?"

"Sometimes. Sometimes not."

"What happens the sometimes when you can?"

"I guess I get sweaty, my heart rate speeds up, my breathing increases, things like that."

I nodded again and thought about that a minute. "I have bloopy blood," I announced. Bud raised his eyebrow at me. "That's what Mom calls it. The doctor calls it something else, but I always forget the word. It means my blood gets tired and weak because it doesn't have enough iron in it to be strong and I do not like spinach like Popeye."

"You're anemic?" Bud asked.

"That's the word, but bloopy blood makes sense. Anyway, when it gets really bloopy and I get so tired I can't play, I have to go to the doctor every week and get my finger stuck so he can look at my blood under a microscope and sometimes he needs to look at a lot of blood or give me some different blood and that means they have to use big needles and tubes and junk and poke around in the veins in my arm. I get really scared when they're going to do that. I get sweaty, my heart beats fast, and I breathe real fast too. I used to get what the nurse called a panic attack. I think that could be kinda like a flashback when you know it's coming. The nurse taught me a trick to stop the attack until after she gets the needle in and then I don't have anything to have an attack about. Wanna learn it?"

"Sure," Bud said, as he squeezed my hand before letting go.

"So you put your fingers on the side of your neck, like this," I demonstrated, "And you move them around a little bit until you can feel your heart thump. Well, go ahead," I prompted. "Can you feel it?"

Bud nodded.

"Now concentrate real hard on the thump. Don't think about anything else, just the thump. Close your eyes and focus on the thump. Count the thumps. If you concentrate on counting the thumps, you can slow them down with your brain power like a superhero. Test your superhero powers and see how slow you can make the thumps. And then just like that," I snapped my fingers, "the scary stuff will be all over with and gone while you were busy paying attention to thumps. See?"

"That's pretty cool," Bud agreed.

"By the way, how come you don't have any friends over besides me and Virgil?"

"I guess I don't have any anymore."

"How come?"

"Just because."

"Because why?"

"Most of them died, okay?"

"Oh. What about friends who didn't go to Vietnam?"

"People change. Let's drop it."

"Okay. I have to go sell poppies now, but I'm so glad we're friends again. I've missed you bunches."

"Sell poppies?" Bud questioned.

"Yeah, you know, the little red, paper flowers that they stick in the Styrofoam crosses when they read the names of the soldiers from around here who died in wars during the show at the Municipal Building on Memorial Day. Me and my friend Macy belong to the Junior Legion Auxiliary on account of both of our grandpas were soldiers in World War II. An auxiliary has to be a girl, but not every girl in school can go to Junior Legion Auxiliary, only girls who have dads or grandpas who were soldiers. We have to go door to door with a bunch of poppies and a coffee can covered up with paper with a slit in the top like a piggy bank and get people to give us a quarter for a poppy. The poppies are to remind people to remember soldiers who died, but I don't know what the money is for. You were a soldier, are you coming to the show at the Municipal Building? I have to wear blue pants and a white shirt with a red ribbon safety pinned across my chest and stand still during the whole thing and it's really long. Then we have to ride in the bus to both the cemeteries here and the cemeteries in the next two towns down the road and stand still again and hold little flags while they read more names, a man plays a trumpet, and then they shoot guns. I don't like that part a bit, because it's sorta sad and a little scary. It takes all day long to go all those places and read all those names and that's an awful long time to stand still, but it's a patriot duty and we have to do it. The first year I did it, my birthday was on the same day. I thought it would never be over. So will you be there?"

"No."

"Why not?"

"I just won't."

"But you were a soldier and it's to honor soldiers."

"They won't be honoring me."

"Why not?"

"They just won't. Trust me."

"But why?"

"Because nobody likes the war I was in or the things I did."

"Well, cheese and crackers," I cussed. "Was it your idea to have a war?"

"No."

"I thought soldiers had to take orders. Did you do stuff in the war without somebody in charge telling you to do it?" I asked.

"No."

"If the war wasn't your idea and you just did what you were told to do, then how come people wouldn't honor you? I swear, sometimes grownups are so dumb, it's a wonder some of them make it to be old enough to be grownups," I declared in disgust. "I'm late. Later, Alligator."

After Macy and I had knocked on all the doors on all the blocks that were ours to cover, we went back the Legion Hall, tuckered out.

We covered the opposite end of town from my block, so we didn't go by Bud's house. I looked on the map to see who had that end. It was assigned to Cindy Watts and Amy Hinkman, my arch nemesis. The Fantastic Four had Dr. Doom and I had Amy Hinkman.

I sucked in a deep breath to be as tall as I could and poked her in the arm. She looked down her nose at me like she was three feet taller instead of only three inches and brushed my hand away like she was swatting mosquitoes. "What?" she hissed.

"Did you go to Bud Nagle's house?"

"Not that it is any of your beeswax, but no, we did not."

"Why not?"

"For one thing, he does not live inside the city limits, and for another thing, we would never go there because I heard he kills children."

"He does not."

"Does so."

"Does not!"

"*That* is what I heard."

"Well, *you* heard wrong. That is a horrible thing to say."

"Well, I heard he was a horrible man. Why are you talking to me, anyway? I told you never to do that unless I talked to you first and I do not *recall* doing that."

"Well, I do not *recall* caring what you tell me," I retorted as I walked away to find the Senior Legion Auxiliary lady in charge of the poppy money.

"Will you be here awhile longer?" I asked.

"Yes. It will take some time to count the money and clean up from the lunch," she replied.

"Okay. Can you save me that box of poppies right there?"

"The whole box?"

"Yes."

"I suppose so."

"Thank you. I'll be back as fast as I can," I promised and ran out the door toward home.

I slammed the door, grabbed a butter knife from the kitchen, raced up the stairs to my room, pried open the bottom of my piggy bank, and started counting. It wasn't enough, but it would have to do. I decided not to take the pennies so there would still be some jingle in the bank if Mom picked it up to dust and anyway, the Legion lady told us to try not to get pennies in our coffee cans, so I didn't think she'd take them. I put all the change in the chest pocket of my overalls so I could ride my bike back to the Hall without spilling any money out of my pockets.

By the time I got back to the Hall, the ladies were loading their cars with casserole dishes and the lady in charge was starting to lock the door.

"Wait. You said I could have the box of leftover poppies," I gasped.

"We do need some for the service on Monday."

"But those were the ones we were supposed to sell. Please."

"Well, do you have money for them?" she asked.

"Yes, right here," I said as I went inside and unbuckled my overalls to dump the pocket full of change on the table.

"How much is there?" she asked.

"Um, I think it's only $4.35, but please can I have them all? It's very important."

"Well, I guess that's a fair price for this bedraggled bunch. I need to get home. Here you go," she said as she handed me the box, scooped the change into one of the empty coffee cans, and pushed me out the door, locking it behind me.

I went back home to my room and carefully straightened out all of the crinkled, green wire stems, tied them together in bunches of ten with pieces of red yarn, and put the bunches in my Easter basket, which was still on my dresser and hadn't been put back in the attic yet.

I wasn't sure Bud would still be home, so I wrote him a note to leave with the basket on his back step. "*I am very sorry about your friends who died. I will remember them for you and honor you when I stand still. Your friend, Jennie P.S. I need the basket back.*"

nineteen

Most years, my birthday was after school let out for the summer, but this year, we had some extra snow days, so my birthday was the last day of school, meaning it was a party even without the party. My friend Shelly and I shared a birthday, so if we were still in school, we had double the treats that day. I liked to go to other kid's birthday parties, but I didn't like to have my own parties because I always worried about whether or not the kids were really having fun at my party. I loved that I had a classmate with a birthday on the same day because she could host the kid party and I could have the fun without the pressure. Shelly's mom usually remembered to have my name put on a cake too and I always had so much fun not worrying I didn't even mind that Shelly got gifts from everyone and only a few of the kids remembered, or were able to convince their parents, that we both had a birthday that day and brought me a gift as well.

My family birthday party was a picnic lunch in the yard on Saturday, complete with macaroni salad and grilled hot dogs. Dad and Papa both complained about the hot dogs. "We raise beef. Why are we eating processed garbage shaped like a stick instead of real meat?"

"Because the birthday girl picks the menu," Mom answered. "When it's your birthday, we can eat steak."

My present from Mom and Dad was the bike I had longed for and lovingly caressed each and every time we had been to Kmart in the past year. The paint was not flat, dull, normal paint. It was sparkly, glistening, sky blue paint that glinted and shined in the sunlight. The bright, white banana seat against the sky blue of the bike made it look like I was sitting on a cloud. White and blue ribbons with silver glitter streamed from the ends of the handle bars, adding even more flash and sparkle to the bike's glory. The white basket on the front completed the look. I just stood in silent awe and gazed at its shimmering splendor. I might have appeared at first glance to be the boy Dad had always wanted, dressed in overalls, tshirts, and cowboy boots, with uncombed hair, skinned knees and elbows, and a perpetual smudge of dirt on my face, but deep down, I was very much a girl and that bike was a beautiful thing to behold.

I had described the bike in detail to Virgil following its discovery and even though he lacked my level of girlish enthusiasm for its beauty, as a show of solidarity, he stood next to me and gave it a respectful moment of silent contemplation before voicing the exact thought I had in my own mind, "You'll be like *Lucy in the Sky with Diamonds,* Squirt."

"Yes. Yes, that's it exactly. I'll be Lucy in the sky with diamonds," I said dreamily as I danced around the bike with my hands swaying in the air, singing, *"Picture yourself in a boat on a river with tangerine trees and marmalade skies. Somebody calls you, you answer quite slowly, a girl with kaleidoscope eyes…Lucy in the sky with diamonds, Lucy in the sky with diamonds."*

"Open your presents from me next. You're going to need one of them right now," said Virgil.

I picked out which ones were his without even looking at the tags because I recognized the wrapping paper as the birthday paper Bert used for gift wrapping presents purchased in the drugstore.

The first gift was the April 1975, #1 issue of *Scooby Doo…Where are you?* comic books, the expensive one, not the one with the cover torn off. As the special first edition, it was triple the size with three stories and one of them was even sort of about South Dakota, *Custard's Next to Last Stand.*

The second gift was a package of four rolls of 50 shot caps. "Are you sure this one is for me?" I asked with a meaningful look at the Lone Ranger holster and cap guns Virgil wore slung about his hips.

"Of course it is, but it wouldn't be any fun if you just shot them all by yourself."

The third gift was the one I needed right then. It was a brand new deck of Bicycle Standard playing cards, the kind Grandpa Oscar used to play poker and solitaire. They came in red or blue. Virgil had gotten me the blue ones so they would match my dream bike, because the cards weren't for playing card games, they were for weaving in between the inner spokes of my bicycle wheels to look cool and to clip with clothespins to the outer edges of the spokes and frame to make motorcycle noises. Virgil smiled as he pulled handfuls of wooden clothespins he'd pilfered from his mom's laundry basket out of his pants pockets and we set to work.

Grandma Mae always baked everyone in the family his or her favorite kind of cake for their birthday. My favorite was German chocolate, triple-decker, layer cake, so Grandma baked two cakes, my special layer cake and a vanilla sheet cake decorated with frosting bluebirds and the candles so there would be enough for everyone. She could have made the German chocolate as a sheet cake so everyone would get a piece, but she knew I liked it as a layer cake better so there would be more places to put the yummy, buttery, brown sugar and coconut frosting.

After the hoopla was over, the presents opened, the cake eaten, the thank-you-kisses doled out, and the relatives gone home, I ran upstairs to get my guns. My guns weren't modern, chintzy, aluminum and plastic, they were Dad's solid metal, Hubley 'Marshal', repeating, roll cap, cap guns from the 1950s, the heavy metal making a much more satisfying bang against the red paper enclosed bit of gunpowder.

I had Dad 'fan' the first dozen caps for me because we liked the sound of the rapid gunfire, but my hands weren't big and strong enough to hit the hammer back fast like that. Besides, I think Dad really liked to do it and it gave Virgil a chance to jerk and flop around, 'dying' from multiple gunshot wounds. After the big death scene, Virgil and I ran around the yard chasing, shooting, and ambushing each other from behind bushes, buildings, and cars through the first roll of caps, then retired to the loft to reload and shoot off the final rolls at a leisurely pace, pausing to blow the smoke off the end of our barrels, trying to make a whooshing whistle sound. We liked the smell of the burnt powder and started sucking up the smoke to blow it out of our mouths, trying quite unsuccessfully to blow smoke rings, until we started to get dizzy and sick to our stomachs. As we lay groaning and holding our queasy bellies, I looked out the window towards Bud's house and asked, "Why didn't he come to the party?"

Virgil smacked his forehead and replied, "I forgot. He said he didn't like crowds, but he gave me something to give to you. I left it in the lilac bush. I'll go get it in a minute, once the smoke in my insides clears."

Virgil came back with my Easter basket. Inside was a package wrapped in butcher paper. When I turned the package over, I gasped in surprise and whispered in astonished wonder, "Oh, Virgil, look, it's me."

"I know. Way cool, huh? Did you know he could draw like that?"

"I didn't know anyone could draw like that."

"It looks real, like I can hear you laughing and you're going to jump off the page and yell, 'You're it.'"

I carefully opened the package, trying not to rip any of the paper so I could save the drawing. Inside was a book, with a cool cartoon drawing on the front, titled *Where the*

Sidewalk Ends, the poems and drawings of Shel Silverstein. I read the first poem aloud to Virgil:

There is a place where the sidewalk ends and before the street begins, and there the grass grows soft and white, and there the sun burns crimson bright, and there the moon-bird rests from his flight, to cool in the peppermint wind.

"Doesn't that sound amazing? You live at the place where the sidewalk ends, Virgil. We need to imagine it like that from now on."

The book was filled with fun and interesting poems that sounded like real kids had imagined them into being. I flipped through the whole thing, occasionally reading one with an illustration that caught my eye or one I thought Virgil would like. When I got to the end, I saw it. Bud had written a note, not on the front cover like most people would, but hidden on the inside of the back cover where no one would notice: *You can do this too, Little Sister. I like your stories better than these. Dream big, dream with your heart, and never let anyone or anything make you give up on your dreams. You have the power to make them come true. Your friend, Bud.*

twenty

The lazy, sweet days of early summer both lasted forever and passed by in the blink of an eye. The land was covered with rich, black dirt and promise and bright, green plants and children, all growing in the sunshine. We ran outside right after breakfast, looking for adventure, and rarely made it back to our own houses until just before the street lights came on.

Virgil and I kept the radio playing everywhere we went. I liked the story songs, Virgil liked songs with good drum parts or guitar riffs he could play along with, and we both liked to sing, making up for what we lacked in talent with enthusiasm.

Janis Joplin's *Me and Bobby McGee* worked for both of us on a warm, June afternoon as we wandered down the road behind Virgil's house toward the United Methodist Cemetery. Virgil played drums on the wooden fence posts with his birthday sticks and I stuck Canadian thistle blossoms in my hair as I sang, "*I pulled my harpoon out of my dirty red bandana. I was playing soft while Bobby sang the blues. Windshield wipers slapping time, I was holding Bobby's hand in mine, we sang every song that driver knew. Freedom's just another word for nothing left to lose. Nothing, it ain't nothing, honey, if it ain't free. Feeling good was easy, Lord, when he sang the blues. You know, feeling good was good enough for me, good enough for me and Bobby McGee.*

From the Kentucky coal mines to the California sun, yeah, Bobby shared the secrets of my soul. Through all kinds of weather, through everything we done, yeah, Bobby, baby kept me from the cold....la da da da la da da la da da da da...

"That one kind of makes me think of us," I said.

"Yeah, kinda. Hey, do you have softball practice this morning?"

"I don't think so. You have a game today though, right?"

"Yeah, late this afternoon. Don't let me forget."

"Okay."

Great Grandma Sadie said it was disrespectful to play in the cemetery, but we didn't disrespect anyone, we kept them company. It was a pretty place too. People grew special flowers and plants there and it was one of the few places around with more than one or two trees. We liked to read the headstones and make up stories about the people and what their lives were like. We played near the really old section on purpose. There were a lot of kids there and we thought they would like it if other kids played near their resting place.

For the pioneers who first settled this land, with no trees for warmth or shelter, living on the barren, windswept plains must have been next to impossible. Each day they survived was a gift, so they counted every one. The headstones from the 1880s read things like 4 years, 7 months, 25 days or 12 years, 2 months, 14 days. Several of them had lambs on top, which always meant a child lay there. The oldest one we could find before 1900 was 58 years, 10 months, 13 days.

My favorite one was a statue of a girl with her arm outstretched and a little bird on her finger. The pedestal read, *"Sweetly sleeps my precious daughter, holy angels guard thy bed. Gently rest in Jesus, darling, till he calls thee from the dead. Etta Jane Hoskins, 1877 – 1886, 9 years, 5 months, 18 days."*

"Virgil, look, Etta is almost exactly the same age you are today."

"Wow. That's sorta spooky. I wonder what happened to her."

"I don't know, but it's awfully sad, all these dead children."

"Hey, Jennie, look at this one, I never noticed it before: *Sally Jean Nelson, Beloved Wife and Mother, 15 years, 4 months, 26 days*. Good gravy, she got married, had a kid, and died and she was younger than my sister, Roberta."

"That's crazy. I guess they didn't have time to be kids because they had to hurry up and live before they died."

"Listen, this is a good cemetery song and it's a story song like you like," Virgil said as *American Pie* by Don McLean began to play.

So bye, bye, Miss American Pie, drove my Chevy to the levy, but the levy was dry and them good ol' boys were drinking whiskey and rye, singing this'll be the day that I die.

"Yeah, turn it up a little."

Did you write the book of love and do you have faith in God above? If the Bible tells you so. Do you believe in rock and roll? Can music save your mortal soul and can you teach me how to dance real slow? Well, I know that you're in love with him, 'cause I saw you dancing in the gym. You both kicked off your shoes. Man, I dig those rhythm and blues. I was a lonely, teenage, bronking buck, with a pink carnation and a pickup truck, but I knew I was out of luck, the day the music died.

"Can you imagine if music really died?" I asked.

"No. I think a world without music would be about the saddest thing ever," Virgil lamented.

"It wouldn't be much of a world at all," I agreed. "Help me pick some wild sunflowers. I'm going to make Etta a crown. She'd like that."

I sat down in the soft, summer grass in front of the little girl with the bird in her hand and started braiding the sunflower stems together as Virgil went in search of more flowers. When I was done, Virgil climbed up on the pedestal and gently placed the crown upon her head. I lay down on my back in the grass so I could look up at the crown of flowers with the sun shining through the petals.

"Ooh, Virgil, come look, there's a circus in the sky," I said as I motioned for Virgil to lie down beside me. "See the elephant?"

"There's a camel," Virgil said as he pointed to a cloud on my right. "And there's a turtle."

"There are turtles in the circus?" I asked with a giggle.

"There are in sky circuses," answered Virgil.

"There's a fat clown, juggling balls."

"Where?"

"Right there."

"How do you figure?"

"Those two blobs are his legs, then his belly and his head, and his arms and the juggling balls are kind of swirling around in a circle."

"You really have to look for that one, Squirt, but I'll give it to ya anyway. The sun's pretty high and my tummy's growling, let's go see if Mom has sandwiches."

"Ooh, then let's go to Great Grandma Sophie's for dessert. She made rhubarb cake yesterday."

"Cool. Why don't we just have lunch there?"

"Because she makes sandwiches out of things like head cheese and cow tongue. I'm not eating a sandwich that can taste me back."

"Ugh, good call."

It was time to mow hay, so we helped Bud get the gunk out from between the triangle shaped blades on the mower sickle bar and grease them up.

"Listen, Bud, it's your song," I said when *Joker* by The Steve Miller Band came on the radio. *"I'm a joker. I'm a smoker. I'm a midnight toker."*

"Bud doesn't tell jokes or smoke, so why is that his song?" asked Virgil.

"He's a midnight toker," I replied.

"What do you think you're talking about?" asked Bud with a scowl.

"I can see your yard from my bedroom window. After it's real dark outside, you stand way out in the middle of the yard and smoke. I can see the little red fire on the end. Why do you just smoke in the middle of the night? Papa and Grandma Cori and Virgil's dad all smoke cigarettes, but they smoke them all day long. I never see you smoke except at night, standing in the yard. Why do you do that?"

"Because I can."

"You're a grownup. When couldn't you?" asked Virgil.

Bud just stared at Virgil and ground his teeth. I could see his jaw sawing back and forth.

"Well? When couldn't you smoke if you wanted to?" Virgil asked again.

"In Vietnam no one could smoke at night," Bud replied.

"Why not?"

Bud didn't answer Virgil, just started to rip the old grass out from between the blades with angry jerks.

Virgil and I shared a look of concern over Bud's bent head. "You know what my dad told me?" I asked. Not expecting a reply, I continued, "My dad told me that you can take away every bit of a nighttime monster's power by talking about him in the day. Monsters can't stand it when you talk about them in the sunshine, because every time you do, they get smaller and weaker, until they just become tiny shadows you can walk right through, with no power to do a single thing to anyone. Isn't that neat, Virgil?"

"Uh huh," Virgil replied in a confused tone.

"Scary thoughts and memories are like nighttime monsters, talk about them in the sunshine and *poof*, they disappear. That's just a neat thing to know," I said.

We worked for a few minutes with nothing but the radio playing softly in the background when I said, "Why couldn't you smoke at night, Bud? You know we'll just keep asking. You might as well tell us."

Bud sighed and said, "Snipers."

"I thought snipe were pretend and snipe hunting was just to fool city kids into sneaking around in the dark with a burlap bag, looking silly."

Bud snorted, "Not snipe, snipers."

"Oh."

"I know," said Virgil, "snipers are soldiers who hide to shoot people by surprise."

"Right," confirmed Bud, "if you smoked a cigarette at night, the enemy could locate you in the dark and shoot you. I smoke at night, out in the open, because I can."

"Oh, so being a midnight toker is a good thing. It's like you're smoking a celebration cigarette. You're home now and you don't have to worry about anyone hurting you anymore. Nice."

Bud just stared at me like he was working something out in his head then he smiled, just a tiny bit, nodded his head, and went back to work.

Sometimes when Mom and Dad wanted to do something 'kidless', they sent us off to Grandma and Grandpa's house to stay overnight. I liked following Mom's younger sisters around. Lynn was in junior high and Kay was home from college for the summer.

"Hey, Grandpa. Whatchyadoin'?"

"Reading the paper."

"Where's Lynn?"

"Lookin' for trouble."

"Where's Kay?"

"Gettin' beautiful."

"Is she going out with Mac?"

"That's usually why you can't use the bathroom in this house for hours on end."

I wandered upstairs to the bathroom. "Hey, Aunt Kay."

"Hey, Jennie-bean," Aunt Kay said as she winked at me in the bathroom mirror. "Hold that tray on your lap, I'm not quite done with it."

I liked to sit on the toilet and watch Aunt Kay get ready for a date. It was fascinating.

"Hand me the eyelash curler."

"Ah…"

"The metal thing, the handle has holes for fingers like scissors."

"Oh, yeah," I handed her the odd looking tool, "Getting beautiful sure is hard work and takes a lot of stuff."

"Jennie Marie Ericson, that is just rude."

"Why? I'm not lying, there's a lot of stuff here."

"Ugh," Aunt Kay sighed in disgust as she opened her eyes wide and leaned close to the mirror, holding her eyelash crimped inside the implement, "Will you get that basket for my curlers?"

I set down the tray of makeup and doodads and reached for the basket, which I held up close to her as she unrolled her hair and dropped the curlers inside. Once they were all out, I stood out in the hallway so I wasn't asphyxiated by AquaNet.

"How do I look?"

"Beautiful. It worked."

"I'm late. I'll pick this up later. Stay out of my stuff," Aunt Kay said as she tapped my nose with her shiny, pink fingernail and swept out of the room in a cloud of perfume.

I stayed out of the bathroom for a little while, but come on, how much temptation is a girl supposed to resist? Aunt Kay very rarely left her beauty tools lying around instead of put away in the cabinet in her bedroom, so chances to mess with them were few and far between.

The eyelash curler was the most complex and therefore intriguing tool. I studied it carefully, turning it every which way. I was too short to see more than the very top of my head in the mirror. That wouldn't work. I set the tool in the sink bowl, climbed up to stand on the toilet seat, then turned around and sat down on the edge of the sink so I could lean my face close to the mirror, thinking that was a required part of the process. Just as I maneuvered my eyelashes in between the metal strips, squeezed my fingers together, and clamped down on the lashes, Grandma hollered up the stairs.

"Jennie? What are you doing up there?"

"Ah…nothing," I hollered back.

"Are you sure?"

"Yep. Nothing's happening up here."

"Why don't you come downstairs and play?"

"Okay."

I thought I had paid close enough attention to what Aunt Kay was doing to be able to do it myself. I apparently forgot to factor in my left-handedness. I must have had it backwards because the ends of my eyelashes were pointed down instead of up. When I tried to spread my fingers open to unclamp it, nothing happened. I couldn't get it to move. It was stuck.

"Jennie? You aren't in your Aunt Kay's things are you?"

"Ah…"

I took my fingers out of the holes, let the curler dangle from my eyelashes, then used both hands to try to open it, lost my balance on the edge of the sink, and bashed my forehead against the mirror.

"Uff-da."

"Do I need to come up there?"

"No, no, I'm coming. Just a minute." I jumped off the sink, slammed the door closed, flushed the toilet for sound effect, and turned on the water. I pulled and tugged and twisted the wicked tool of torture.

"Get your fanny down here," Grandpa yelled from the diningroom.

"Coming," I hollered back as I yanked on the curler one last time, ripping it off my eye, along with most of my eyelashes. "Son of a biscuit baker!" I cussed aloud at the burning pain. I stumbled down the stairs, holding my hand over my throbbing, bleeding, lash-less eyelid.

I was willing to listen to Grandma's scolding in order to get some ice wrapped in a dishtowel and a little sympathy for my wounds. Grandpa didn't even look up from his newspaper when I moaned as I walked by on my way to the kitchen. "Got caught like a mouse in a trap, didn't ya?"

It was a warm, summer evening, so I got to sleep in the hammock on the screened in back porch. If I bumped my hip against the wall, I could get the hammock to swing while I listened to the toads croak and the crickets chirp and imagined I was young Jim Hawkins, sailing the high seas on his way to Treasure Island to find the hidden pirate booty.

I was deep into my fantasy adventure when Mac and Kay came up the walk and for just a minute, I thought it might be Blind Pew come to get me.

When Kay and Mac stopped to stand on the porch steps with their heads bent close together, I jumped out of the hammock.

"Hey, guys."

Kay jerked her head back in surprise and smacked it against the door jam.

"Grandpa told me to watch out for you and be sure to say hello just as soon as I saw you."

"I'm sure he did," grumbled Kay.

"Did you bring your guitar, Mac?" I asked eagerly.

"Sorry, I didn't know my backup singer would be here tonight."

"Dang it. I brought the tambourine out and everything." I liked to be in Mac's band. *Love Potion No. 9* was my favorite number. I sang backup vocals, played tambourine, and danced the Swim and the Pony while Mac played the guitar and sang lead. I even had a dramatic tambourine solo between *I held my nose and closed my eyes* and *I took a drink*, along with a big finish.

"Maybe next time," said Mac as he ruffled my hair then held my chin in his hand to turn my face towards the streetlight, "What happened to your eye, Ikette?"

"I think I hear Grandma calling me. See ya."

twenty-one

"I'm bored," I lamented late one afternoon.

"No one will stop you from weeding the garden," Mom answered.

"I'm not that bored."

"Well, there is always that option, so I don't want to hear about it."

I wandered outside and drew a round target with smaller and smaller circles in the driveway gravel with a stick, then sat back in the grass and pitched rocks, trying to hit a bull's eye. I was thinking about what to do next when I heard a noise that didn't fit. It sounded like someone sniffling. I looked around, saw Virgil in the loft window, and went to investigate.

"Why didn't you signal me? I didn't know you were out here."

Virgil shrugged his shoulders.

"Are you crying?" I asked.

"No," Virgil mumbled as he rubbed his face with the back of his hand.

"Whatsamatter?"

"Nothing."

"Are you sure?"

"Yes! Nothing's the matter!" Virgil yelled.

I stepped back. Virgil never yelled at me. I sat down on the straw bale and kept quiet, trying to gauge what he would say or do next, but I was never very good at keeping quiet.

"Is there something I can do to fix it?" I asked.

"No, Jennie, you can't fix it. Nobody can fix it. Just shut up, why don't you?"

"Okay." I sat back and tried not to be upset. I had learned long ago that lots of kids had secret hurts they suffered through in silence. They didn't tell grownups because oftentimes grownups were the ones causing the pain and they didn't talk about it with other kids because they knew most kids were just as powerless to stop the hurt as they were. Why share it if it would only make someone else feel hurt for you and recognize his or her own helplessness?

After several quiet moments contemplating that sobering truth, I said, "Hey, I know, why don't we go camping?"

"Because we don't have a tent or sleeping bags or any way to get anywhere."

"We don't need any of those things. We can go imagination camping right here in the yard and Mom is great at imagicating things."

"I don't think imagicating is a word, Squirt."

"Sure it is. It's like a compound word. It's a combination of imagine, magic, and fabricate, which Dad says means invent or build or create. Mom is really good at helping me make props for imagination games. She's an excellent imagicator. I just tell her what I want to imagine about and she finds stuff around the house to help me make it more real. Mom's cool like that. C'mon, let's go, it'll be fun, I promise."

Mom proved her imagicating skills with a couple blankets and some cinder blocks. She made each of us our own tent by throwing a blanket over the clothesline and staking out both sides with a block on each corner. She laid old sheets on the grass inside each tent and told us to get a pillow and blanket from our beds.

Mom saw us gathering sticks for a campfire and said, "Do not light up that fire or I will light up your behinds."

"What are we going to do for light then?" I asked.

"Make lanterns," Mom replied.

"How?"

"It'll be fun," Mom said, then went inside and came back out with two Mason jars and a nail. Mom used the nail to poke air holes in the metal jar lids, then handed one to each of us. "When the sun starts to set, the fireflies will come out. You catch them and put them in your jars and they will light them up like lanterns."

"Cool."

Virgil and I sat Indian-style in our tent doorways, facing each other.

"It's time for the imagination part. Where are we camping?" I asked. "You get to pick."

"Um...the waterfall."

"What waterfall?"

"The one from our song." Virgil tapped the tune out with his drumsticks on the Mason jar and sang, "*Standing in the sunlight laughing, hiding behind a rainbow's wall, slipping and a sliding, all along the waterfall with you, my brown-eyed girl.*"

"Excellent. The waterfall runs into a little lake and we're camping beside it."

"I'm getting hungry. Let's catch some fish for supper. We'll catch rainbow trout."

"Rainbow trout? Is that a real kind of fish?"

"Yeah. We can catch them and cook them over the fire."

"No way," I protested.

"What do you mean?"

"We are *not* cooking rainbows."

"That's just what they're called. They're regular old fish and we are so cooking them."

"No, we are not. You can't eat something that sounds as pretty and magical as rainbow trout," I insisted with a pout.

"Fine," Virgil sighed. "What are we going to eat then?"

"Berries. There will be berries beside the lake."

"How do you know they're not poisonous?"

"There would not be poisonous berries beside a magical waterfall with a rainbow wall and rainbow trout."

"Why not?"

"Because you can't get killed imagination camping."

"Well, there'd better be a lot of non-poisonous berries because I'm really hungry and I was all ready to eat fish."

"Don't worry. There is an endless supply of very tasty berries at our campsite."

"Look, I just saw a firefly blink." We ran all around my yard and Virgil's for hours catching fireflies and filling our jars. We lay down on our bellies in our tents with our chins on our hands and our noses next to the glass to watch our lanterns flicker. At first, the blinking lights were neat, but as we looked closer, we saw the fireflies bashing themselves against the sides of the jars, over and over, trying to escape. We studied the fireflies in silence for a few minutes then I looked around my jar at Virgil to see if he was thinking what I was thinking.

Virgil looked back at me and said, "You know, I really don't think we need any lanterns."

"Yeah," I agreed, "there are plenty of stars out tonight. We can see just fine by the starlight."

Without further discussion, Virgil and I both opened our jars and shook them to let the fireflies know they were free to go and watched them fly away, blinking their thank yous back at us.

We lay down on our backs this time with the tops of our heads touching and traced connect-the-dots shapes in the sky using our fingers to draw imaginary lines between stars. When we ran out of shapes, Virgil turned the radio back on, but we continued to watch the sky, waiting for a shooting star.

"That's it," I said as I heard the opening piano chords of a familiar song, "That's my song for you, Virgil, always and forever." I reached up above my head for Virgil's hand and held it tight as the notes of the song drifted on the night air: *Sometimes in our lives we all have pain, we all have sorrow, but if we are wise, we know that there's always tomorrow. Lean on me when you're not strong and I'll be your friend, I'll help you carry on for it won't be long 'til I'm gonna need somebody to lean on. Please, swallow your pride if I have things you need to borrow for no one can fill those of your needs that you won't let show…If there is a load you have to bear that you can't carry, I'm right up the road, I'll share your load, if you just call me. Call me, if you need a friend. Call me.*

twenty-two

Virgil whistled to signal his arrival in the yard and I raced out to meet him, laughing as I climbed on my sky bike and kicked up the kickstand because *Born To Be Wild* by Steppenwolf was just coming on the radio. Virgil lifted the back end of his bike off the ground and I reached out and spun his back tire so his playing cards made motorcycle noises as we belted out, *"Get your motor running. Head out on the highway. Looking for adventure in whatever comes our way."*

You never knew what you could get into on a bright, summer day. We were taking the bikes because we had a lot of places to go. First, we were headed to my friend Jamie's house on the other side of town for a job picking dandelions. Jamie's dad was paying us fifty cents each to fill a grocery sack with dandelions so he could make dandelion wine. We picked them all over town as people were happy to get rid of them in the yards and ditches when they were still yellow flowers before they went to seed. We were experienced pickers this year and knew to just pop the heads off without pulling the stems so we could avoid having to handle them twice.

The kitchen smelled great with the first load cooking in the pot when we delivered the second load. Jamie's dad boiled the dandelion heads with lemons, oranges, and spices before distilling it. After much begging and pleading, we had each gotten a sip of last year's finished product and though it smelled good at the start, the taste at the end crinkled our noses, dried out our tongues, and burned our throats.

When handing us our pay in shiny quarters, Jamie's dad suggested we might want to put one quarter in our savings. We looked at each other for half a second to consider his suggestion before announcing in unison, "Nah, let's go to Bert's."

That fifty cents was burning a hole in our pockets. We couldn't get to Bert's fast enough. Fifty cents could go a long way at Bert's, providing hours of sugar-fueled entertainment.

We burst through Bert's door with a jingle of bells, each trying to decide where to head first.

"Well, hello there," Bert greeted us as he turned his stool and looked up from reading the paper on the counter, "What can I do you for this fine day?"

"We're shopping today, Bert, and we've got cash on the barrelhead," I announced.

"You do? Well, now. What did you do to earn all that jingle in your pocket?"

"We picked dandelions for Dad," answered Jamie.

"Will makes the finest dandelion wine in all the land, must be because he's got good pickers."

"Must be," agreed Virgil.

I got a strawberry popsicle out of the white cooler at the end of the counter and laid down on the floor in the corner to sort through the box of comic books with the covers torn off. Jamie headed for the back to look in the toy aisle. Virgil picked up a pack of candy cigarettes and sucked on one, trying to look cool while he flipped through the car and motorcycle magazines on the rack.

I polished off my popsicle, put my stack of selected back issue comic books on the counter, and asked Bert for a sack. Bert handed over one of the tiny paper sacks we used for penny candy and I sat down in front of the candy counter to count out the penny candy on the floor and fill up my sack with Sixlets, Pixie Sticks, Jawbreakers, and Bazooka bubble gum.

Jamie came out of the back with a red and white striped hoola hoop. "Bert, can I test it out first?" she asked.

"That'd be fine, Jamie, but try not to scuff it up in case you change your mind," responded Bert.

"Bert, Mom says I need to get a haircut today, but I'm not paying for it with my fifty cents. It's Mom's idea, so you need to put it on her tab," said Virgil.

"All right, young man, have a seat," Bert said as he put a wooden pop bottle crate upside down on top of the barber chair so Virgil would sit up higher. Bert shook out a long, white cape and fastened it around Virgil's neck. I leaned up against the door jamb to the barber shop room, sucking on a Slow Poke, to watch the show. Bert did a mean buzz cut with an impressive flick of his wrists.

After our shopping trip concluded, we headed back home so Virgil could get ready for his baseball game.

As we pedaled down the street, *Cat's in the Cradle* by Harry Chapin came on the radio.

And the cat's in the cradle and the silver spoon, Little Boy Blue and The Man in the Moon. "When ya comin' home, Dad?" "I don't know when, but we'll get together then, son, ya know we'll have a good time then."

Well, my son turned 10 just the other day, he said, "Thanks for the ball Dad, come on let's play. Can ya teach me to throw?" I said, "Not today, I got a lot to do." He said, "That's ok," and then walked away, but his smile never dimmed, he said, "I'm gonna be like him, yeah, ya know I'm gonna be like him."

Virgil switched off the radio.

"Hey, I like that one, even though it makes me a little sad," I said.

"Dad's trucking today," said Virgil.

"Oh," I replied as I realized what was bothering him. "You know, Mom said Bud used to play baseball. Let's go see if he'll give you some pointers and maybe go to the game."

"Hey, Bud."

"Hey, Thing 1 and Thing 2."

"Ha. That's funny, Bud. You should try to be funny more often."

"Mom said you played baseball. Can you show Virgil some stuff? His dad is trucking and my dad went to look at some equipment somewhere. He's got a game today, can you come with us?"

"I don't know."

"C'mon, Bud. Please?"

"I don't play anymore," Bud said as he raised his bum arm up as far as he could.

"But you still know how. You can teach us what you know. You just have to talk for that."

"Let's practice here and try it out," said Virgil as he started looking around the outside of the machine shed.

"What are you looking for?" I asked.

"Something to use for a bat," Virgil replied.

"You can find a real one next to the dresser in the room at the top of the stairs," said Bud as he washed his hands at the well.

Virgil took off for the house.

"Toss me the ball, Little Sister." Bud reached out and plucked the ball out of the air.

"Don't you need a glove?" I asked.

"I think I'm good," said Bud. "What position do you play?"

"Well, I played right field last year, but I got stuck."

"Stuck?"

"Yeah, I got kinda bored because no balls ever came my way and I started poking around a gopher hole. Somehow, my foot got stuck in the hole and then, wouldn't you know, a ball came my way. It was the darndest luck."

Bud dropped his head and shook it.

"I know, who woulda thought a ball would come right when was I stuck? I was good and stuck too. I'm not a very good runner either on account of I've got puny lungs because I was born early and they didn't have time to finish growing, so I don't get enough breath. Coach said we had to think of a position where I didn't have to run a lot and I had to pay attention all the time and not get distracted or I'd get beaned by the ball, so this year we're trying catcher. I'm not great yet, but I'm getting lots better. My friend Macy is the pitcher and she makes me help her practice all the time."

"It's hard to change the size of my lungs, but Dad said if I play smart and build up other muscles, I won't have to worry about running. I squeeze a ball while I watch cartoons to make my hand stronger and I scoop grain and corn and clean up the bin site to make my arms stronger so I can throw and hit the ball farther and then I don't have to run so much."

"Good idea. Say, I thought you were left-handed."

"Well, I am, but Dad wasn't sure sports were really my thing and left-handed gloves are expensive, so I just used his old glove when I started and now I'm used to throwing right-handed. I bat left-handed though, because that's another play-smart-don't-run thing. Pitchers don't like left-handed batters, I'm already real short, and I squat down even shorter when I bat, so I have a teeny, tiny strike zone that's hard to hit. I get walked a lot."

Virgil came running back out to the yard with a Louisville Slugger in his hand. "This is an awesome bat, Bud. Did you win all those trophies up there?"

"The bat too," answered Bud.

"Cool."

"Batter up."

Virgil held the bat up to his shoulder and I squatted behind him.

"Both of you watch the ball all the way in," said Bud. "Choke up a little, Virgil, and lift your back elbow. Open up your glove a little, Jennie, and keep your eyes on the ball 'til it lands in your glove."

Bud worked with us for an hour and we learned a lot.

"We're gonna be late. The diamond's all the way across town. You'll have to come with us now, Bud."

"I'll drop you off."

"If you're already there, you might just as well stay. It'll be fun. Mr. Decker's grilling beer brats at the concession stand today and the Jayceette ladies are running it. They always bring Rice Krispie bars. Virgil needs a sideline coach. Please? Pretty please with sugar on top?"

"It's a great day for a ballgame. What else are you gonna do? You have to take us anyway. I won't get to play if I'm late. C'mon."

"All right. Get in the truck."

"C'mon, Bud," I said as I drug him by the hand toward the bleachers. "I need to sit on the top so I can see." The crowd parted like the Red Sea as we climbed the bleachers.

"Well, Bud Nagle. It's good to see you out and about."

"Where you been keeping yourself, Bud?"

"Long time no see, Bud."

"Just like the old days when you boys were state champions, huh, Bud?"

Bud just nodded his head at people as we passed by.

"See, Bud, everyone is happy you're home," I said as I patted his knee.

twenty-three

South Dakota made the national news on June 26, 1975 and for several days thereafter. We were mentioned on every channel because of the shootout at the Pine Ridge Indian Reservation. Someone on The Ridge, as the locals called it, had apparently shot and killed two FBI agents. The Indians and the FBI were having an old-fashioned standoff.

"Why do they just keep showing people standing around on the road?" I asked Dad.

"I guess they're playing chicken, waiting to see who blinks first."

I lived in a state with nine Indian reservations, but I didn't know much about them. For the most part, Indians and white people each stayed close to home and didn't mingle.

Mom had an old 45 of the song *Running Bear*. I would listen to it over and over, even though every single time I played it, I cried, because Running Bear and Little White Dove both jumped in the raging river in order to be together and they drowned. I loved the song and knew every word, but even I doubted that could be considered knowledge of Indian culture.

Pretty much all I knew about The Ridge in particular was that it was the poorest place in the state and lots of kids there didn't have warm clothes or enough to eat. Every year around Thanksgiving, my Sunday school class would collect money, mittens, hats, and winter coats to box up and mail to the kids on The Ridge.

"Why are there so many Indian Reservations here, Dad?"

"Well, because back when Europeans settled this land, many tribes roamed this area following the buffalo across the prairie. The Indians were already up here and this state has several areas of crappy land you can't do anything with, so they stuck the Indians on it. If this country has anything to be truly ashamed about, it's their treatment of the Indians. Before we came along, spreading disease and taking land, millions of Indians lived here in relative harmony. That was a long time ago though and what's done is done. Our family and others like us get to own the land and farm here now and that's the way it is."

"Are you coming out to the farm for the 4ᵗʰ of July?" I asked Virgil.

"Yeah, I don't think we're doing anything else."

Papa loved the 4ᵗʰ of July. He bought out fireworks stands and we spent hours and hours shooting them off. He even rigged up a shoot for them made out of a fence post driver so they would go higher and could be shot more accurately.

Dad helped us with all kinds of inventive ways to shoot firecrackers and I twirled cases of sparklers in the night sky.

Great Grandma Sophie made gallons of homemade ice cream. Everyone in the family took a turn at turning the crank, as it was an all day long process, and I licked the dashers. We made messy, enormous ice cream sundaes to eat while we watched the fireworks show.

"Is Bud coming?" asked Virgil.

"No. I asked him, but he said he was going camping in Canada for some peace and quiet. He doesn't like crowds and I think loud noises bother him."

Ed's Grocery had two aisles jam-packed with almost everything a big grocery store in the city carried. Ed knew every item in the store at all times. We tried to stump him by asking for the least commonly used ingredients we could think of, but he would always shuffle down the aisle and reappear with the item in his hand, as if by magic.

Ed's wife Aileen spent hours every day dusting the cans and boxes with a giant feather duster made of huge, brownish-gray feathers that seemed as if they must have come from a pterodactyl or at the very least, a great, monstrous bird not naturally found in the wilds of South Dakota.

Grandma Cori clerked the occasional afternoon in the store and I liked to keep her company. She let me use Aileen's feather duster, but after a few minutes, it made me sneeze. I must have been allergic to pterodactyl.

I went outside to get some fresh air and wandered into the hardware store next door to look at the pretty paint sample display and maybe catch some old guy gossip as older men often gathered to sit in folding chairs back near the cash register counter to drink coffee, smoke, and play cards.

"I heard he showed up at the baseball game with that little Ericson girl."

My ears perked up when I heard my name.

"Think he's all there? He doesn't talk to anyone but those kids."

"I heard he was the only guy in the platoon to make it out alive."

"Someone said he was out in the bush on his own for a week."

"He's probably good and messed up in the head."

"Safe to say he's got a screw or two loose, but seems like a decent enough guy."

"Even though he's a cripple, he still looks strong as an ox. I'd hate for him to go off half cocked."

I burst out of the aisle with, "Hey! Don't talk about people like that! He's not crazy!"

"Pipe down. You watch how you speak to your elders, Missy, or someone will tan your hide."

"Well, you shouldn't talk mean about people," I replied. "He went through some bad and scary stuff and got lost for awhile, but he found the road home so he could remember what he was like as a kid before the bad stuff happened and heal his heart. You need to welcome him home and be his friends instead of talking about him behind his back." I turned and ran out of the store before I could catch heck from any of the men. I was sure my parents would hear about my disrespectful outburst and I might yet get my hide tanned, but it seemed like it was worth it.

twenty-four

The long-awaited harvest was finally upon us. Dad lived for harvest. He loved driving the combine and bringing in the crops. He couldn't wait until the dew was off in the morning so he could start and he stayed out in the field until dark and sometimes beyond.

Mom, Grandma Cori, and Great Grandma Sophie took turns packing lunches and snacks and Mom and I delivered them to the fields. I would often stay and join Dad for the afternoon.

My favorite field lunch was cold, minced roast beef salad on thick slabs of homemade bread, potato chips, bread and butter pickles, carrot cake bars with cream cheese frosting, and iced lemonade served in a Mason jar, dripping wet with condensation. Those meals with Dad in the cramped, dirty, dust and chaff-filled, combine cab, bouncing through the field, eating up acres, were some of the most enjoyable meals of my life.

"Can I drive, Dad?" I asked.

Dad scooted back in his seat and held out his left arm so I'd have room to climb over the auger lever and slide under the steering wheel to lean against the edge of the seat and stand between his legs. I used to sit on his lap, but this year I was big enough to drive by myself without Dad's hand on the steering wheel with me, though I had to stand up to be able to see over the steering wheel.

"Don't get us stuck in a gumbo hole."

"I won't, Dad."

"Straighten it up. Whoa. Too far. Get the windrow back in the middle of the header. That's it. Now just hold it there. You should be good without turning too much 'til the end of this row."

I could steer by myself, but Dad had to operate the controls for the elevation and tilt angle of the header and the speed. I couldn't do that many things at one time.

"Think you can make the corner?"

"Um…I'll try it."

"Okay. I'm slowing down. Make a wide corner. Turn the wheel just a little bit to your left so the windrow slides over to the right side. There you go. Now, crank it to the right."

Wheat flew up and over the edge of the header. "Whoa, missed it by *that* much," Dad said as he grabbed the wheel to straighten us out.

Driving was fun, but it required lots of concentration. I usually didn't last very long.

I sat on the floor, right up next to the window, and stared at the heads of wheat being gobbled up by the giant machine until I felt dizzy and hypnotized.

I moved back up to my seat on the metal box next to Dad and said, "Let's sing." Dad and I liked to sing the songs Dad remembered from children's choir when he was a boy.

I danced around in the tiny square of floor space in the cab and did the hand motions as we sang, "*Six little ducks that I once knew, fat ones, skinny ones, fair ones too, but the one little duck, with the feather on his back, he led the others with a quack, quack, quack, quack, quack, quack, quack, quack, quack. He led the others with a quack, quack, quack. Down to the river they would go, wibble, wobble, wibble, wobble, to and fro, but the one little duck, with the feather on his back, he led the others with a quack, quack, quack.*"

Our favorite was *Kookaburra*, even though Dad only remembered one verse. We sang at the top of our lungs, over and over, "*Kookaburra sits in the old gum tree. Merry, merry king of the bush is he. Laugh, kookaburra, laugh, kookaburra, gay your life must be."*

I went on lunch trips and go-fer trips, moving the trucks and equipment from one field to the next, with Mom and Grandma and I went on parts trips with Papa. Whenever something broke down and needed parts from Hannity's Implement in the next town up the road in order to be fixed, Papa would swing by the house and holler, "Who's riding shotgun?" I would drop whatever I was doing and run to the truck, for there was nothing better on a hot, summer day than an ice cold bottle of Nesbitt's strawberry pop and as far as I knew, the big red and white pop machine in the back corner of Hannity's Implement was the only source in the universe for strawberry flavored Nesbitt's. If the part wasn't a huge emergency, I'd have two bottles of strawberry pop, one the minute we arrived, and one while Papa had a quick snort with Mr. Hannity in the bar and grill next door.

Wheat needs a moisture content around fifteen percent in order to be harvested or it will get moldy when stored. Dad could usually tell whether or not the wheat was dry enough just by tasting it. He would pick a few heads of wheat, rub and roll the heads together between his hands to get the chaff off and get to the wheat kernels, then pop them in his mouth and chew. If the kernels were hard and crunchy all the way through, the moisture content was probably okay. If the kernels were soft or chewy at all, the grain was too wet and would need to dry in the sun a few more days.

Dad's taste tester was pretty good, but if it was too close to call, he would run a couple of rounds through the combine, dip an old coffee can full of grain out of the hopper, and take it to the grain elevator to be tested.

One afternoon following a thunderstorm, Dad and I stood in the elevator office lobby and chatted with several men waiting for their samples to be run. Bud came in the elevator as well, but stood in the corner by the door, quietly waiting his turn. Several of the other men greeted him by name or nodded their heads in his direction. Bud nodded back, but stayed neared the door and didn't engage in any conversations.

I wandered over to stand beside Bud and smiled up at him, but he didn't say anything. The testing machine was loud and sounded a little like the rain pounding on the tin patches of the machine shed had sounded. I studied Bud's face. It had become expressionless, he stared straight ahead without blinking, his skin paled, and beads of sweat were beginning to collect on his forehead and upper lip.

Dad had gotten his test results and headed for the door, "Coming, Punkin'?" he asked me.

"Um...I'll be just a minute, Dad. Bud and I have some business to discuss. I'm going to do a job for him."

"Okay, then, Little Entrepreneur. Don't be long, we need to get in a few acres today," Dad said as he nodded at Bud and headed out the door.

I wrapped the fingers of my left hand around Bud's wrist and felt around for his pulse. His heart was beating fast. I tapped the thumps of Bud's heartbeat out on the top of his hand with the index finger of my right hand, hoping he would remember the stop-the-panic-attack trick. I didn't talk, just kept tapping the rhythm of the thumps. After a few minutes, the thumps started to slow then Bud took a deep breath and cracked his neck. "Thank you, Squirt," he whispered.

"You need to pay me and Virgil to scoop up the grain around your auger or in the bottom of your bins. We can put the grain in the back of your pickup and you can dump it here so they'll pay you for it and then you can pay us. We do good work. See ya later, Alligator."

twenty-five

"Dad, did you know there was such a thing as an allowance?"

"You don't say."

"It's when parents give their kids money."

"What for?"

"Just because it's what they do."

"Huh."

"Don't you think that's a good idea?"

"Not really."

"C'mon, Dad. I think I should get an allowance too."

"Most people work to earn money."

"I do work."

"Do you?"

"Yes. I do lots of work around here."

"Lots? Really, Jennie?"

"Well…some. I do some work around here."

"And I believe you are well compensated."

"How's that?"

"I let you live here rent free and Mom cooks you meals and buys you clothes that she then washes for you."

"How about if I do a little more than some work? Then can I have an allowance?"

"Well, when people work to earn money, they often have a contract that defines the scope of work. Let's negotiate your contract. Go find some paper and a pencil."

I ran off to find the requested items then plopped back down at the kitchen table, pencil at the ready. "Shoot."

"Okay, I'll dictate the draft of your contract."

"What's dictate?"

"I tell you what it should say and you write it down."

"Got it."

"I, Jennie Ericson, do solemnly swear…"

"How do you spell 'solemnly'?"

"Erase 'do' and write 'promise'. You know how to spell that?"

"Yes. 'I, Jennie Ericson, promise'…"

"'That I will complete the following tasks'…then list the things you will do to earn your allowance."

"Make my bed, pick up my toys…"

"What else?" Dad prompted when I paused.

"Ah, pick up and put away my clothes."

"And?"

"I need more?"

"I thought you said you were going to do more than some work. You're already compensated for those things on the list so far with room and board. Keep going."

"Um, set the table and dry the dishes."

"Uh huh."

"More?"

"I'm still only seeing some. You're going to have to go above and beyond."

My list of tasks seemed quite extensive by the time we finished.

"But what will I get for all of that?"

"We're getting to the monetary compensation portion of the agreement now. At the bottom of the task list write, 'in exchange for the sum of twenty-five cents per week, payable in cash each Saturday morning.'"

"No way," I protested. "I'm not doing that whole list of stuff for only twenty-five cents."

"You're not?"

"Nuh uh."

"How about thirty cents?"

"Nuthin' doing, Dad. A dollar."

"No dice, Jennie. Fifty cents."

"Seventy-five."

"Sold, to the blonde in the red t-shirt," said Dad.

Three weeks later, just before school started, Dad asked if I wanted to go to the sale barn with him. I loved the sale barn, so I jumped at the chance.

The trailer was empty, so I knew we weren't selling anything and asked, "What're we getting, Dad?"

"I just thought we'd take a look around," Dad said.

We parked the truck and wandered around the parking lot and the paddocks outside the sale barn. Dad stopped to talk to an old man leading a short, black horse.

"How much are ya hoping to get for her?" Dad asked.

I thought he was just making conversation, but the man responded and, wonder of wonders, Dad made a counter offer. As the men started to dicker, I held my breath. Dad was buying a pony. I couldn't believe my ears. Aunt Kay and Mac had given me a beautiful hardcover copy of *Black Beauty*, with a brightly colored painting on the cover and gold trimmed pages, for my birthday. I had read it cover to cover three times already. I desperately wanted a horse of my own, but never in a million years did I dream Dad would just buy a pony for no special reason.

Dad walked with the man and the horse, back to a beat up old truck and trailer in the parking lot. The man opened the trailer door and led a much younger, prancing, red filly out.

Dad got his checkbook out of his back pocket, laid it on the hood of the pickup, and wrote out a check that he handed to the old man then handed me the rope attached to the halter of the calm, black horse and tried to settle the filly before walking back to our trailer.

"That's it?" I asked. "We didn't even go inside the sale barn or hear the auctioneer. Do these horses belong to us? We're taking them home right now?"

"Yep," said Dad.

"Really and truly, Dad?"

"Really and truly, Jennie Marie."

"But, it's not my birthday or Christmas or anything."

"Every girl needs a horse of her very own. You told me so just the other day. Besides, you're paying for them."

"I am?"

"Yep."

We loaded the horses in the trailer and climbed in the pickup cab.

"How can I pay for horses?" I asked. "I only have $5.86 in my piggy bank."

Dad picked up the tablet and calculator on the dash, took the pen out of his pocket, and said, "Let me explain a little something called compounding interest." Dad wrote down a bunch of figures and explained accounting principles I did not understand for several minutes.

"What's the bottom line, Dad?"

"The bottom line, Jennie, is that you will not be eligible to receive an allowance again until approximately the year 2006."

I grabbed Dad's calculator, punched in 2006 and subtracted the year I was born. "I'll be 40 years old."

"That's about the size of it," Dad said as he started the truck and pulled out of the lot towards home.

Bud's combine had broken down before his crops were in and proved to be unfixable. Dad heard about his plight before our trip to the sale barn and bartered harvesting services in exchange for boarding the horse he hoped to find.

In a stunning display of originality, I named my horses Black Beauty and Ginger.

twenty-six

This school year something new and exciting was happening in our family. Mom was going to school too. She was going to college to become a nurse. At first, I thought it was weird. None of my friends' parents went to college. None of my friends' moms had jobs either. They all stayed home to take care of kids or help on the farm. Then I thought about how Mom and Dad were always telling me I could be anything I wanted to be when I grew up, whatever I dreamed of doing, I could do if I studied and worked hard to make the dream come true. I realized Mom wasn't just a mom, she was a girl who had dreams too. I didn't think about it being weird after that, I just thought about being proud of her for studying and working extra hard to be both a mom and a nurse.

Mom knew my friends' moms just took care of their kids and didn't go to college though and she was a little worried about it.

"We're going shopping for some special clothes for school, Jennie."

"Okay," I said with some confusion.

We only shopped at one store and we only bought one brand of clothes. The clothes were called *Garanimals*. They all had tags shaped like animals. The trick was that if you matched the animal tags, the outfit matched. For example, a shirt with a tiger tag was meant to be worn with pants with a tiger tag. If you wore a shirt with a tiger tag and pants with a monkey tag, your outfit did not match and did not look good. Tigers and monkeys together would look like you didn't know how to dress yourself.

As we hung up the new clothes, Mom said, "Now these special clothes are the only clothes I want you to wear to school this year, Jennie."

"How come?"

"Because you sometimes have questionable fashion sense and I'm going to school in the city, so I'm going to have to leave early some mornings. You're going to have to get yourself dressed and off to school and Dad won't pay any attention to what you're wearing. I want to make sure you look decent. I don't want anyone to think I'm a bad mother and you're being neglected, looking like a mismatched ragamuffin. You need to promise me you will comb your hair every day too and you will keep combing it until you get out all the snarls. People are already going to be talking about me, please don't give them more to talk about."

"Okay, Mom. I promise. I will not go to school looking like a neglected, snarly-haired, mismatched ragamuffin."

It was tough for Virgil and me to get to school on time. There were so many possible distractions along the way.

Old Mr. Bendenally met us at my mailbox most mornings as we started on our way. He gave us each a stick of Black Jack gum. Black Jack gum turned your mouth black and your spit purple-ish-gray when you chewed it, which was cool, but it tasted revoltingly like black licorice, a bad idea for gum in my opinion. It was very nice of him to think of us though and we accepted each stick and chewed most of them for a few minutes anyway, just in case it was an acquired taste we might someday come to enjoy beyond its purple spit capabilities.

The haunted house across the street from the United Methodist Church looked spooky even in the morning sunshine. It was a huge, gray stone house with broken green shutters and shingles banging in the wind. We both wanted to run past the house so no ghost or goblin would have time to reach out and snatch us off the street. If any other kids came along about that time though, we had to at least fake brave and slow down. Kids would often double-dog-dare each other to walk down the broken sidewalk, up the rickety porch stairs, hold a hand against the big, scarred door, and count to twenty.

We weren't allowed to go inside Pat's Place, the local bar, but in the mornings, we liked to take a peek inside. If we both stepped up to stand on the arms of the bench out front at the same time, it wouldn't tip over and we could cup our hands around our eyes and see in the window. It was always dark and smoky inside, with just one light glowing way back by the bar, illuminating Pat as he leaned over the bar and read the paper. Pat was a muscular guy, who always wore jeans and a t-shirt with a pack of cigarettes rolled up in his shirt sleeve. We liked to think he looked like a gangster and we made up stories about the shady deals that went down inside the bar.

Papa's sister, Aunt Toots, was the Post Mistress. If we promised not to touch anything, she would let us watch her work. You wouldn't necessarily guess it just by looking at her, but Aunt Toots could move like Flash Gordon when sorting the mail. You couldn't even see her hands, they moved so fast. We begged repeatedly to be allowed to sort the mail into boxes, but Aunt Toots informed us that any unauthorized individual handling the mail was committing a Federal offense, which simply could not be allowed on her watch. We could do things like put water in the little dish that held the wet sponge people used to lick their stamps or pin the new FBI Wanted posters to the bulletin board in the lobby or use the big, manual, postage date stamper on a blank piece of paper if we promised not to stamp anything else.

We often stopped at the bank to get pink paper penny wrappers and round suckers with looped shaped sticks.

Years before our time, the Catholic Hall was a car dealership, so the building had many unique features, including ramps and landings for displaying cars. Virgil aspired to be Evel Knievel, so he would practice by getting a good run at it, peddling furiously up the ramp and across the landing, to hurl himself into space, jumping over the steps on the other side. I admired his ambitions. After all, I had my very own Evel Knievel doll with a white spandex, caped jumpsuit and a Gumby-like, poseable body on a motorcycle that really moved by itself after you ran the wheels backwards, however, I was not particularly coordinated and recognized at an early age that my body was not Gumby-like. I waited patiently at the stop sign to pick up the pieces or call for help in the case that Virgil crashed on approach or his landing was less than stellar.

Virgil's Grandma Jo sometimes worked the morning shift and did the baking at Lucy's Lunchette and Laundromat. If Grandma Jo was in, we'd swing by and grab an apple fritter or a long John for the road.

We held the school record for the most number of tardies and sometimes had to stay in for recess or stay late in after school detention as a result, but it just didn't seem reasonable to expect us to ignore all of the countless things that could snare our attention on an eight-block journey.

Virgil and I boogied into Bud's yard singing along with Elton John and making up dance steps to the *Crocodile Rock*.

I remember when rock was young. Me and Suzie had so much fun, holding hands and skimming stones. Had an old gold Chevy and a place of my own, but the biggest kick I ever got was doing a thing called the Crocodile Rock. While the other kids were rocking round the clock, we were hopping and bopping to the Crocodile Rock.

Bud shook his head at us.

"Hey, Bud."

"Hey, Short Stuff."

"Whatchadoin?"

"Nothing much."

"We came to see if you had any chicken wire we could have. We ran out."

"What do you need chicken wire for?"

"Our class float for the Homecoming parade. You're coming to the football game, right?"

"Nah."

"C'mon, Bud, you have to come to the Homecoming game. Please? We want you to see our float in the parade. We're the last ones before Mr. Benton's convertible with the king and queen in the back seat. You *have* to come. Virgil's going to get to bring Simon on the float. They're going to be the stars."

"Simon too, huh?" Simon Sez was Virgil's ventriloquist dummy. Virgil got him for Christmas and was always working on new material for his shows. He practiced a lot. You almost couldn't see his lips move anymore.

"Yep. Isn't that cool? You have to be there."

"Maybe."

"It's going to be my biggest audience ever, Bud. You can't miss it."

Bud did come to the game in time to see Virgil and Simon on our float. Once the parade was over, I went to stand beside him and watch the game while I drank my hot chocolate. Bud didn't talk much, but everyone who walked past made some comment about the good old days when Bud played ball.

"Wow, Bud. You must have been really good," I said.

"I wasn't bad." Bud crossed his arms and continued watching the game. Pretty soon, he started muttering things under his breath.

"What?"

Bud shook his head. After a couple of minutes, he started in again with the muttering.

"Who are you talking to?"

"Them. They're going to…no, no, not that play, not…ugh."

"You should stop by practice and help them too like you did me and Virgil playing baseball. You're like a football celebrity. I'm sure they'd listen to your advice."

Bud didn't respond, but he did start making his suggestions out loud so someone might hear him and eventually he even cheered when the boys had a good play.

By the time the game was over, Bud didn't just nod to the people who spoke to him, he started talking back. A group of men gathered around him, each adding a piece of the story, reminiscing about a homecoming game when Bud was the quarterback. Soon even Bud couldn't help but join in, recalling the events of another, long ago Friday night under the lights. As I saw him raise his hand, pantomiming throwing a pass as he spoke, I smiled. Bud was having a homecoming of his own.

twenty-seven

The cattle were still in a rented summer pasture a couple of miles east of Bud's. Dad wanted to check on the grass supply to see if they could stay a couple more weeks before herding them back to the farm. He suggested Virgil and I come along and we ride the horses to check the cattle cowboy style.

Virgil and I were all for that idea. We loved to play cowboy. Beauty was docile as a lamb. In fact, it took a good deal of encouragement just to get her to move. Since she was never in any big hurry to go anywhere, it wasn't a huge challenge to stay on her and Virgil and I chose to ride bareback for comfort's sake.

Dad rode Ginger, who was almost saddle broken, but not quite. She still needed some practice tolerating a rider for an extended period of time as she quickly became bored with plodding along and wanted to run free.

The ride through Bud's pasture and the wheat stubble beyond before reaching the pasture where the cattle were held was fairly uneventful. Ginger shied at a passing jackrabbit, but settled down again after only a few seconds of Dad's wrangling.

The cattle liked to congregate under the tiny patch of shade trees near the creek that ran through the middle of the pasture and we headed that direction to get a head count to be sure they were all still inside the fence and none had escaped in search of greener pastures.

I'm not sure what happened, but apparently Ginger was done being docile and wanted to be free of Dad's weight on her back. She went wild, bucking and kicking like a rodeo bronc. Dad held on for what would have probably been a qualifying time in a rodeo, but was finally unseated.

Beauty stood by and chewed grass, completely uninterested in Ginger's display of poor behavior, but Ginger wasn't finished. After tossing Dad to the ground, she raced in circles, taunting him and seeming to throw back her head and laugh at his futile attempts to catch hold of her reins.

Ginger looked back at Dad as she raced away from his grasping hand and in doing so, she lost sight of where she was headed and ran into Beauty's back end.

Beauty had had enough of Ginger's shenanigans at that point and bucked up just her rear end in an attempt to kick Ginger with both of her back hooves.

Beauty had never done anything like that and we weren't expecting it. When Beauty kicked up her rear end, Virgil flew up in the air, over my head, turning summersaults like he was in a cartoon. He flew so far I thought for sure he would be killed when he hit the ground. I was anxiously watching Virgil and not paying attention to what I was doing at all. As a result, when Beauty started to run, I wasn't holding on with my legs or holding the reins and I slid off her back to the ground, striking a rock at just the right angle to snap the bone in my thigh clean in half.

As I hadn't yet tried to move, I wasn't aware that anything was wrong with me. Dad had raced to Virgil's side, thinking he would be gravely injured. Virgil had the air knocked out of him, but got up without a scratch. Dad helped him knock the dust off his jeans and looked around to see which direction the horses had headed.

I started to get up and couldn't help but let out a blood-curdling scream as the most intense pain I had ever experienced in my life raced through my body and I fell back to the ground.

I panted in agony as the wave of pain rolled through me.

"Baby, what's wrong? Where are you hurt?" Dad asked as he felt my head, arms, and sides. I couldn't answer him. I could only pant as I waited for the pain wave to roll out through my head. Dad felt my legs from the feet up and when he brushed my right thigh, I screamed again, Dad's hand stopped, his face paled, and he swore, "Holy…" unable to say anything more.

"Okay, Baby. It's okay. It's going to be okay, just don't move. Lie still," Dad told me, then turned to Virgil and gripped his shoulders to be sure he had his full attention. "Virgil, listen to me. We can't catch the horses. You have to get help. I need you to run as fast as you can to Bud's house. You find Bud and tell him Jennie is hurt. Her leg is broken. Bud was a medic in the army. He'll know what to do. You tell Bud to meet us at the crossroads then go home and see if your mom can go with you to tell Trish and watch Julie or take her to one of the grandmas. Can you do that, Virgil?"

"Yes, sir."

"Good boy. Now run." Virgil took off like a jackrabbit.

"Okay, Sweetie. We have to get you to the road so Bud can pick us up. I'm going to have to pick you up and carry you. I'll be just as careful as I can, but you're going to have to be brave. Can you be brave, Honey?"

"Yes, Dad," I whispered.

"I'm going to have to hold my hand on the break. It's going to hurt, but you're a tough cookie, right, First Born?"

"Yes, Dad," I agreed.

"Here we go," Dad said as he gently slid one hand under my legs, the other around my shoulders, and stood up. I sucked in my breath, clenched my teeth, and clutched Dad's shirt in my fists. I twisted and squeezed the fabric of Dad's shirt so hard the fabric started to tear.

Dad walked as carefully as he could through the pasture. After covering about half the distance to the road, I sobbed, "Please stop, Daddy. Please stop walking."

Dad stopped, kissed my forehead, and laid his cheek against the top of my head while I cried into his chest. After a few minutes, Dad whispered, "We have to keep going, Baby. I'm sorry."

"But it hurts so bad, Daddy. It hurts so bad when we move," I sobbed.

"I know, Sweetness. I know it does, but we have to get you to the hospital so the doctors can fix it. You need to be strong for just a little while longer. Can you do that, Jennie? Can you be my big, strong girl a little longer?"

I wiped my nose and my tears on his shirt and said, "Yes, Dad."

"That's my girl," he praised as he began walking again.

When we reached the road, Dad leaned over the fence and held me until I touched the ground, even though the barbed wire ripped his shirt and scratched his stomach. He let go of the break, pulled his arms out from under me, and stood to climb over the fence. As he did so, the ends of the bone separated. With no support, the muscle and tissue oozed out through the void and wiggled like a snake. "Daddy! Daddy!" I screeched in horror at the gruesome and unnatural sight.

Dad leapt over the fence and dropped to his knees beside me, trying to figure out where to put his hands.

Bud's pickup fishtailed on the loose gravel as he slammed on the brakes to stop. He jumped out of the truck with a broom, a yardstick, and a handful of dishtowels.

"Hey, Little Sister. What kind of scrape have you gotten into this time?" Bud asked as he broke the broom over his knee and started ripping dishtowels into strips.

Dad had decided to hold his hands on both sides of my leg to try to stop the wriggling flesh.

I was in full-on panic mode, panting like a carsick dog.

"How come you're not using your superpowers? Find the thumps. C'mon, Jennie," Bud encouraged as he demonstrated finding the pulse in his neck with his fingers and looked me straight in the eye. "Find the thumps and concentrate, Jennie. Slow 'em down. That's right. Deep breath. Focus on the thumps. Thatta' girl."

Bud pushed on my foot a little then put the broom handle and the yardstick on either side of my leg and motioned for Dad to hold them in place. He quickly knotted several strips of dishtowel around my leg to hold the splints in place.

"Keep counting thumps, Jennie. How slow can you go?" asked Bud as he grabbed a pile of blankets and pillows out of the front seat and arranged them in the bed of the pickup.

"Okay, Little Sister, Dad's going to get in the truck and I'm going to hand you up to him."

"Can you do that with your bad arm?" I asked.

"Don't you worry about me. I can't do chin ups, but I can carry a little bit of a thing like you."

Bud was able to lift me, but his arm shook like a leaf in the breeze and beads of sweat ran down his face.

They loaded me in the truck and put the pillows under my leg. Bud slowly turned around at the corner and headed toward home. Dad held my head in his lap with one arm under both of mine and across my chest to hold me in place. I clutched the blanket and turned my face to let Dad's jeans soak up my tears as he stroked my hair back with his hand.

We had to move one more time to go from the truck bed to the backseat of the car. I wore Huffy brand boy's jeans Grandma Cori ordered for me from the Sears catalog. They were the toughest jeans made. During the forty mile trip to the hospital, my leg swelled so much the stitches on the heavy duty seams started to pop.

After we settled in the emergency room, the orthopedic surgeon came to see me and announced, "The strangest coincidence, there's a 34 year old man in the room next door with the exact same break, nice of you both to coordinate my day so well."

"The bone pieces have moved so that they are overlapping each other. I'm afraid the only way to line them back up again is the old-fashioned way. We're going to have to pull. The other guy got here before you did, so his pain killers have had a few more minutes to do their job. We'll take care of him first and then come get you straightened out, okay?"

"How you doing, Tough Girl?" Dad asked as he brushed the hair from my forehead.

"Okay. It doesn't hurt much if I don't move."

Just then, the man next door yelled so loud you could hear him around the block. Dad's eyes grew wide as saucers and his face paled to a chalky white. Mom sagged into a chair by the bed like her legs quit working.

I swallowed hard and said, "Don't worry, Dad. You didn't raise a sissy girl. When it's my turn, I'll suck it up."

Dad turned and walked out of the room.

"Mom?" I asked with uncertainty.

Mom gripped my hand, "Oh, Jennie. You don't have to suck it up. That's just for little hurts. You've been so strong and brave. Dad just needs some air."

Dad didn't come back into the room and Mom didn't see him in the hallway, but I was determined he wouldn't hear me yell like that man had.

A big man in blue pajamas came into the room.

"Hey there, Little One. My name is Bob."

"Hi, Bob."

"I'm just going to hold on to you so you don't slide off the bed, okay?"

"Okay."

"Now, I'm hard of hearing, so you just yell as loud as you need to, all right?" Bob said as he bent over with his head next to mine and held me under my armpits with his arms bent up at the elbow to be sure he couldn't lose his hold.

The doctor held my ankle and counted to three. I squeezed my eyes shut tight, gritted my teeth, and gripped the bed rails. I didn't make a sound, but I passed out cold.

twenty-eight

The orthopedic doctor didn't have any other patients who were kids, so instead of being in the pediatric ward with other kids, I was on the orthopedic floor with adults.

I was in a double room in the bed near the window, farthest from the door. Any visitors had to walk all the way into the room, past my roommate's bed, and around the partially pulled curtain before being able to see me.

I was pretty dopey for a couple of days after surgery. Just as I started to snap out of it, Bud and Virgil came to visit me. I was so happy to see them. I was bored out of my skull and lonely as could be.

They both stopped abruptly at the foot of my bed. Neither said a word, just studied the contraption to which I was tethered.

"Hey, guys," I said.

Virgil whispered, "Oh, Squirt."

"It's okay. It's not near as bad as it looks. Just don't bump the bed, huh?"

"I'm going to go find some coffee," said Bud.

Virgil sat down in the chair with a thump. "It looks pretty bad, Squirt."

I shrugged. "It doesn't hurt that much unless I move."

"What is all this stuff?"

"It's called traction. My leg broke in half, but they didn't want to mess around with the bone and use a screw or something to hold it together until it heals because I'm still growing. There isn't anything holding the broken pieces together. Tendons are kind of like rubber bands stretched around your bones. If the bone is broken in half, the tendons might squish the pieces together so they slip and slide next to each other again instead of end to end where they're supposed to be. C'mon over on this side and look," I said as I pointed to my knee, "They pounded a steel rod through the end of that big bone down by my knee. The rod has little holes on the end. See, those cables are tied through the holes. The cables go up there, through the pulleys, across the thing on the top, down the bars on the end, and through those weights. The weights on the cables pull on my leg and stretch the rubber band tendons so the bone stays in the right spot. As the bones knit together more, they'll take off weights, but right now there are a lot of weights and it hurts most all the time."

"How long do you have to stay trussed up like that?"

"They won't tell me. I think a long time. Did you know Bud was a medic in the army?"

"No, did you?"

"Nuh uh."

"He was kinda weird about it when I went to get him."

"What happened?"

"I was awful tired by the time I got there. It was a long run. I pounded on the door and yelled for him. I was yelling, 'Help! Help! Jennie's hurt. We need help!' I was so tired I fell down on ground and leaned against the door trying to think where he might be and when I looked up, he was just standing there in the driveway with that spacey daymare look on his face. I had to scream at him and shake and hit him before he looked at me and saw me."

"Then what?"

"Then he kind of snapped out of it. I told him the story as fast as I could and he told me to go up and get the blankets and pillows off the bed, then he took off after you."

"Thank you for running all that way to get help, Virgil."

Virgil shrugged. "You would have done the same for me, Squirt. Have you seen your Papa yet?"

"No. You're my first visitor besides Mom and Dad. I think anyway. I've been sleeping a lot 'til today."

"He was real upset."

"Did you see him?"

Virgil nodded.

"How do you know he was upset?"

"He's the one who went out and found the horses. Beauty was still in the pasture, but Ginger had jumped the fence. I don't know where he found her, but he tied her to the back of the truck to bring her back, and put her in Bud's corral. Then he went and got a gun and came back to shoot her. Bud went out and stopped him. He told him it was just an accident and you'd be mighty upset if he pulled the trigger."

"Oh, no," I whispered.

Virgil cleared his throat. "Teacher said she'd visit at the end of the week and bring you your assignments. We've all been working on a surprise for you in art. Don't ask me what it is, 'cause I'm not gonna tell."

Virgil told me the news from school, a funny story from recess, and a few new jokes he'd come up with for Simon to tell.

Bud came back in with his gimme cap in his hand, cleared his throat, and said, "They been treating you okay?"

"Yeah. The nurses are real nice. It's awful lonely though. Thank you for visiting and for bringing Virgil."

"Sure thing, Little Sister. Well. We'd better head out."

"Will you come back when you can stay longer? Please?" I pleaded.

"You bet," said Bud.

"Later, Alligator," Virgil said as they walked away.

"After while, Crocodile," I said to their backs as I choked back a sob.

Mom visited every day, before her classes started, during her lunch break, and after classes were over. I memorized her schedule and watched the clock on the wall, counting down the minutes before she came each time.

Even though it was an eighty mile round trip, Dad came every evening to tell me about his day, tuck me in, and kiss me goodnight. The first day, the nurse came in to say visiting hours were over, but I begged and pleaded with her, "Please, please, let him stay until I fall asleep. Please? He'll be very quiet and won't disturb anyone else. You won't even know he's here. Right, Dad? Please." The nurse relented in the face of my puppy dog look and a note was made at the station that Dad was allowed to stay beyond normal visiting hours.

It was hard for me to go to sleep at the hospital. There were so many unfamiliar, scary noises and I didn't want Dad to leave. He stroked my hair, rubbed my cheek with his thumb, and even recited the baby rocking poem. Dad was just out of high school when I was born. He'd never been around babies and he didn't know any nursery rhymes or lullabies, so he recited a poem by Edgar Allen Poe that he had learned in English class to rock me to sleep:

Gaily bedight, a gallant knight, in sunshine and in shadow, had journeyed long, singing a song, in search of Eldorado. But he grew old, this knight so bold, and o'er his heart a shadow fell as he found no spot of ground that looked like Eldorado. And as his strength failed him at length, he met a pilgrim shadow, "Shadow," said he, "where can it be, this land of Eldorado?" "Over the mountains of the moon, down the Valley of the Shadow, ride, boldly ride," the shade replied, "if you seek for Eldorado."

The baby rocking poem never failed to calm me and make my eyelids heavy.

After several nights though, I got to wondering how long Dad stayed, so one night, I just pretended to be asleep. When I started breathing evenly, Dad held my hand in both of his, laid his head on the edge of the bed, and cried. He cried for the longest time, whispering, "I'm sorry, Baby. I'm so, so sorry."

It was awful. I didn't know what to do. I wanted to open my eyes and tell him it was just an accident, it wasn't anyone's fault, he didn't do anything to be sorry about, but I was paralyzed by the sound of his cries and couldn't seem to make myself move or speak. I never just pretended to be asleep again. I tried to be happy and excited when Dad came and never told him how lonely I was or how much my leg hurt and my heart ached.

Bud returned on his own several days after bringing Virgil to see me. I was able to sit up a little higher by then and didn't have to just stare at the ceiling all day. I could eat by myself and set things on the bedside table that moved up and down.

Bud brought a big bag from Kmart and held a cherry Icee in his hand.

"Oh, Bud! Is that Icee for me? I *love* cherry Icees from Kmart."

"So I heard."

"What's in the bag?" I asked between long slurps of Icee.

"Entertainment," answered Bud. He pulled out a red, transistor radio and a big package of batteries and set them on the table. "I couldn't find one with wings," he apologized.

"Oh, Bud. Thank you, thank you. I've missed Virgil's radio so much."

Bud sat down in the chair by the bed and pulled a long box out of the bag.

"Battleship!"

"Yep," said Bud. We set up our ships, readied our pegs, and started shooting.

"B7," I announced triumphantly.

Bud just groaned.

"That's it? You have to say it."

"What?"

"When I get one, you can't just groan, you have to say it."

"Say what?"

"_You sunk my battleship_, like on the commercial."

"No."

"You have to, it's part of the game."

Bud just raised his eyebrow at me.

Bud didn't let me win. He said I had to learn to work for what I wanted, just like every other schmuck. After he packed away the game inside my nightstand, he put batteries in the radio and turned it on for me.

"How did you know just what I needed?"

"I've been where you are."

"Stuck in a hospital bed?"

"Yep."

"When you got hurt in the bush?"

"How'd you know about that?"

I shrugged. "I hear stuff. What happened?"

Bud cleared his throat and started bouncing his leg, but didn't answer me.

"Where you really a medic in the army like Dad said?"

"Yeah. I was in medical school when I joined up instead."

"What's a platoon?"

Bud cleared his throat again. "It's what they call a group of soldiers."

"Were you really the only one who didn't die?"

Bud was quiet for a long time and I didn't think he would answer me.

"Yeah."

That was so sad it made my heart hurt. "Is that when you were stuck in the hospital?"

"Yeah."

"For how long?"

"Six months."

"That long? Did you have anyone to visit you and bring entertainment?"

"No."

"I'm sorry. You should have called home to tell people where you were. People from home would have come to visit you. All kinds of people come to visit me. Look there, Bert brought me a whole big box of comic books with the covers torn off. The Esther Circle ladies from church visit me when they visit the people in the nursing home and they crocheted me a blanket. Grownups I've never even talked to before have come to see me and some of them have brought their grandkids or their nieces and nephews who are kids I know from school. "

"I was in the hospital far away."

"Everybody should have visitors. When I get out, I'm going to remember to visit soldiers in the hospital who don't have visitors."

Bud nodded his head and we both sat back and listened to the radio, each lost in our own thoughts. A long song I had heard only once before, *A Hard Rain's Gonna Fall* by Bob Dylan, started to play. I remembered the song because even though I didn't understand what it all meant, it painted pictures in my head and made me sad.

Oh, where have you been, my blue-eyed son? And where have you been, my darling young one?

I've stumbled on the side of twelve misty mountains. I've walked and I've crawled on six crooked highways. I've stepped in the middle of seven sad forests. I've been out in front of a dozen dead oceans. I've been ten thousand miles in the mouth of a graveyard. And it's a hard, it's a hard, it's a hard, it's a hard, it's a hard rain a-gonna fall.

Oh, what did you see, my blue eyed son? And what did you see, my darling young one?

Bud reached out and switched it off.

"Whatsamatter?"

"You don't need to hear that. I want you to hold on to pretty pictures of the world for as long as you can," Bud said.

twenty-nine

"I need you to do me a favor, Virgil," I said while we played cards.

"What's that? Do you have any 8s?" Virgil asked.

"Go fish. I need you take over my jobs," I replied.

"What jobs?"

"I need you to be Great Grandma Sophie's doughnut hole roller. It's time to butcher hogs. Mr. Schmidt will be bringing her a bucket of lard. That means it's time to make doughnuts on Saturdays. She's going to need help."

"What do I have to do?"

"It's real easy. When Grandma cuts the doughnuts, there's a ball in the middle that gets left behind. She fries those pieces to make doughnut holes and she needs someone to roll the warm holes in sugar. Do you have any 3s?"

"Go fish. I like the sound of that job. What else?"

"Pheasant hunting starts next weekend. Uncle Whitey will be here with his friends. You have to be the dog since I can't do it."

Uncle Whitey was Papa's brother and an important salesman for International Harvester. He even sold a tractor to Elvis Presley once when he lived in Memphis, Tennessee. He and Aunt Lena traveled around the country and lived in mysterious, far away places, but they always came home for Christmas Eve and a week-long stay in the summer, showering us with gifts, souvenirs, and stories from their adventures. Nearly every year, Uncle Whitey brought his biggest clients home to go pheasant hunting and it was my job to be the dog. That meant that I walked the bottom of the Big Ditch while Uncle Whitey and his guests walked the ridges above and waited for me to flush the birds out of their hiding spots, then I picked up the birds when they fell from the sky and carried them in a bird hanger on my belt. The metal bird hangers looked a little like key holes. They had a big spot at the top where the bird's head fit and then they got skinny so that just the bird's neck fit down in the slot and the head blocked them from falling out. I didn't like that part of being the dog. I didn't look down and tried to pretend the bird hanger wasn't there. Uncle Whitey was proud of me for doing a good job and bragged about me to the other men, so I didn't want to disappoint him and act like a sissy about the poor, dead birds.

"That'd be an okay job too. I like Uncle Whitey. He teaches me magic tricks."

"Yeah and his friends will give you money and presents. It's a good deal."

I was happy Virgil was going to take care of things for me, but I was so sad I couldn't do my jobs myself that I got a big lump in my throat I couldn't swallow.

My first grade teacher, who taught me to read and supplied me with books from other libraries after I had read all of the books in our classroom, had heard that it was hard for me to hold books up high enough to read for long, so she got a cassette recorder, recorded story time for me, and sent the tapes with my regular teacher when she brought my assignments. They were reading the *Little House on the Prairie* books. I listened to the tapes over and over until the lady in the bed next to me yelled for me to turn it off already.

One day, Virgil sent me a tape too. His Aunt Maggie had given him a tape recorder because she said he was a born performer and she wanted him to be able to practice and follow his dream.

Because he could use lots of different voices, he recorded Ray Stevens' *The Streak* for me.

Hello everyone, this is your Action News reporter with all the news that is news across the nation, on the scene at the supermarket. There seems to have been some disturbance here. Pardon me, sir, did you see what happened?

Yeah, I did. I's standin' over there by the tomaters and here he comes, runnin' through the pole beans, through the fruits n' vegetables, nekked as a jaybird, n' I hollered over t'Ethel, I said, "Don't look, Ethel!" n' it's too late, she'd already been incensed.

Here he comes. Looka dat, looka dat. There he goes. Looka dat, looka dat. And he ain't wearing no clothes. Whoa, yes they call him The Streak.

I laughed so hard I got the hiccups. Even my grouchy roommate asked me to play it again.

I had never been away from home for more than one night and then it was only to stay with my grandparents or my friends and Mom and Dad were just a few miles away at most. I had been in the hospital over a month and the doctor said it would be at least another month, closer to two, before my leg would be healed.

I couldn't stand it anymore. When Mom came for her last visit of the day, I started to cry. "Momma, *please* find a way for me come home. Please. I can't do it anymore. I tried and tried to suck it up and be a brave, strong girl, but I just want to come home. Please, Momma. I'll do anything. If you take me home, I promise I'll be good. I will just lay in my bed and I won't move a single muscle, not one. My bones can knit at home. Please, Momma. Please don't make me stay here all by my lonesome anymore. Please, Momma," I sobbed inconsolably.

"Oh, Jennie, it's not up to me."

"Isn't there some way? Can't you think of something? You can fix it, Mom. You're good at fixing things. Please, please fix it so I can come home," I wailed.

"Hush. Hush now," Mom crooned as she bent over the bed and held me. I cried and cried until I almost made myself sick. Desperately trying to calm me down, Mom started singing softly, *"Hush little baby, don't say a word, Momma's gonna buy you a mocking bird. If that mocking bird don't sing, Momma's gonna buy you a diamond ring. If that diamond ring turns brass, Momma's gonna buy you a looking glass. If that looking glass gets broke, Momma's gonna buy you a billy goat. If that billy goat runs away, Momma's gonna buy you a brand new day."*

thirty

Mom did find a way to fix it so that I could go home, or so it seemed to me. The doctor agreed that I could go home if they put me in a body cast. They warned me it would be uncomfortable, but I was willing to do anything.

They put me to sleep again to take off the traction and put on the cast. The cast was made of plaster and went from my chest all the way down to my ankles. It took several days just to dry and it weighed far more than I did. Mom and Dad rented a hospital bed they put in the livingroom and a wheel chair with the arms removed so I could move around a little bit. I still couldn't go anywhere, but at least I was home.

I couldn't play outside, but my friends and family could visit me every day and I could watch what I wanted on TV. Dad watched *Rocky and Bullwinkle* and *Mighty Mouse* with me early in the morning before he went to do chores.

In the afternoons, Virgil came over and watched *Captain 11* with me. We always recited the intro along with the announcer: *One man in each century is given the power to control time. The man chosen to receive this power is carefully selected. He must be kind. He must be fair. He must be brave. You have fulfilled these requirements and we, of the Outer Galaxies, designate to you, the wisdom of Solomon and the strength of Atlas. You are Captain 11!*

Captain 11 was filmed in Sioux Falls and real kids got to be in the show. Kids could just go to the studio and they would get to sit in the little bleachers on the set and be part of the Captain's crew. All the kids said their names and what town they were from and played guessing games to win prizes from the toy chest. Kids who went on the show for their birthdays got to operate the Captain's control panel and flip the switches that made the cartoons play. At the end of the show, the kids played Freezeburg. They all got up from their seats and looked at the cameras. The Captain would tell them to wave one hand, then both hands, then both hands and one foot, then both hands and both feet, and then he would yell, "Freeze," and all the kids would have to try to stay just like they were without moving a muscle. The camera would pan back and forth trying to catch kids twitching or falling down. It was our lifelong dream to appear on *Captain 11*.

I thought the Captain looked quite a bit like Dave Dedrick, the weatherman on KELO-TV, and I mentioned this observation to Dad. Dad said most superheroes from outer space had similar backgrounds, so Captain 11 was a lot like Superman. Superman had to be reporter Clark Kent during the day and Captain 11 had to be weatherman Dave Dedrick. It made sense to me.

Virgil and his dummy, Simon Sez performed all of their new material for me. Some of it was funny, some not so much.

"How many tickles does it take to make an octopus laugh?" asked Virgil.

"Idunno," said Simon.

"Ten tickles," said Virgil and paused for a dramatic moment of silence. "Get it?"

"No," said Simon.

"Ten tickles. An octopus has tentacles."

Simon shook his head.

"That was good," I said. "You're getting better."

Virgil set Simon in his box and sorted through the stack of records he had brought over. He found the one he wanted and set it on the turntable. If you moved the needle all the way over to the right until it clicked, it took a second to pop back over and move down to the record, so Virgil had time to jump up on the ottoman, grab the handle of the mop he had standing in the bucket to be used as his microphone, and announce, "Live from the Livingroom, it's Glen Campbell!" He then pushed the mop away and grabbed his tennis racket serving as a guitar and sang, *"I've been walkin' these streets so long, singin' the same old song. I know every crack in these dirty sidewalks of Broadway, where hustle's the name of the game and nice guys get washed way like the snow and the rain. There's been a load of compromisin' on the road to my horizon, but I'm gonna be where the lights are shinin' on me. Like a rhinestone cowboy, riding out on a horse in a star-spangled rodeo. Like a rhinestone cowboy, getting cards and letters from people I don't even know and offers comin' over the phone..."*

"Yay!" I cheered as he bowed low.

"My sisters really feel sorry for you. They actually gave me permission to bring over some of their records and I didn't have sneak them out."

"Cool. What did you bring?"

"I brought all the story songs I could find, just like you like. I've got *Bad Bad Leroy Brown* by Jim Croce, *One Tin Soldier* by The Original Caste, *Leader of the Pack* by The Shangris-La, *Wildfire* by Michael Martin Murphy, and a new one they just got called *Blind Man in the Bleachers* by Kenny Starr." Virgil put the stack of records on the stereo, then plopped down in the bean bag chair near my bed to listen.

We liked *Bad Bad Leroy Brown* because Leroy Brown was Encyclopedia Brown's real name, it said the word damn, and we thought the chorus was fun to sing, *"He's bad, bad, Leroy Brown, baddest man in the whole damn town, badder than old King Kong, meaner than a junkyard dog."*

I closed my eyes and just listened to *One Tin Soldier* so I could see the story in my head like a movie.

Listen children to a story that was written long ago, 'bout a kingdom on a mountain and the valley folk below...turned the stone and looked beneath it, 'Peace on Earth' was all it said.

Mom had *Leader of the Pack* too, so I had it memorized. I even had a dance routine for it. "You're going to have to be the backup singer girls, Virgil."

"No way."

"Please?"

"Huh uh."

"Virgil, I have a broken leg."

"Oh, for Pete's sake. Fine."

"I met him at the candy store," I crooned, *"He turned around and smiled at me. You get the picture?"*

"Yes, we see," sang Virgil in a falsetto voice.

"That's when I fell for," drama-filled breath, *"the Leader of the Pack."*

"Vroom, vroom," Virgil made appropriate motorcycle noises.

As *Wildfire* played, Virgil asked, "I don't get it. Why does this one make you cry? It's just about a girl chasing a horse, right?"

"Aren't you listening to the story?" I replied. "The horse runs away in a blizzard and gets lost, the girl goes out looking for it, and they both freeze to death."

"Oh. Well, it's a really long song. I guess I don't pay attention all the way to the end."

We'd never heard *Blind Man in the Bleachers* before, so we listened carefully.

He's just the blind man in the bleachers to the local home town fans and he sits beneath the speakers, way back in the stands, and he listens to the play by play. He's just waiting for one name. He wants to hear his son get in the game.

But the boy's just not a hero, he's strictly second team, though he runs each night for touchdowns in his father's sweetest dreams. He's gonna be a star some day, though you might never tell, but the blind man in the bleachers knows he will.

And the last game of the season is a Friday night at home and no one knows the reason, but the blind man didn't come. And his boy looks kinda nervous, sometimes turns around and stares, just as though he sees the old man sittin' there.

The local boys are tryin', but they slowly lose their will. Another player's down and now he's carried from the field. At halftime in the locker room, the kid goes off alone and no one sees him talkin' on the phone.

The game's already started when he gets back to the team and half the crowd can hear his coach yell, 'Where the hell you been?' 'Just gettin' ready for the second half,' is all he'll say, 'cause now you're gonna let me in to play.'

Without another word, he turns and runs into the game and through the silence on the field, loudspeakers call his name. It'll make the local papers, how the team came from behind when they saw him playin' his heart to win.

And when the game was over, the coach asked him to tell what was it he was thinkin' of that made him play so well. 'You knew my dad was blind,' he said, 'tonight he passed away. It's the first time that my father's seen me play.'

The record player clicked off and Virgil and I sat in silence, each wiping our tears away.

"That is the saddest song I have ever heard in my entire life," I said.

"Uh huh," Virgil agreed.

thirty-one

I made Mom and Dad promise me that they would talk Bud into coming to our house for Thanksgiving dinner.

"He won't want to do it, but remind him that it's a little girl who's asking…a little girl with a broken leg…in a *body* cast, for Pete's sake. Even Bud can't say no to something that pitiful," I declared.

"You're really milking this for all it's worth, aren't you, First Born?"

"Yep. Use what you got," I replied.

Bud did come to Thanksgiving dinner. He mostly stood off in the corner, trying to blend in with the curtains, but he did talk a little farming with Dad, gave Aunt Lynn some pointers on drawing portraits, asked Grandma Mae what kind of birds she saw in the winter, and talked with Great Grandma Sophie about when she and his parents were young.

I asked to say the blessing, so everyone gathered around my bed in the livingroom. "Dear Lord," I prayed, "Thank you for giving us so many family and friends nearby. Thank you for the new brother or sister you are sending to our family in the spring. Thank you for making bones that knit back together when they break and for sending me home, to the place where I can feel love all around me to help me finish healing. And most especially, Lord, thank you for helping our friend Bud find the road home, back to the place where he was a boy, the place where he can feel love all around him to help him finish healing too. Amen."

The room was quiet for several seconds until Grandpa clapped his hands and said, "I hear that turkey gobbling my name."

Virgil came over for dessert. I had three helpings of Grandma Mae's frozen cranberry salad with pineapple and marshmallows.

"Bud, guess what."

"What?"

"You have to come to Christmas Eve church service."

"I do?"

"Yes."

"Why is that?"

"Because the children are going to do the nativity scene at Christmas Eve church service this year instead of a couple weeks before because my Sunday school teacher wanted to be sure I got to play a part. I'll for sure have my cast off by Christmas. I have plenty of time to study my lines and learn a big part, so I get to be Hark. Virgil is going to be a shepherd and Julie is going to be his sheep."

"I can't use the hook on my staff to make Julie go the right way though. Don't you think I should be able to? That's why shepherds had hooks, you know," said Virgil.

"Wait," said Bud, "I got the shepherd and the sheep, but who are you again?"

"Hark," I replied.

"I don't remember any names in the nativity scene other than Joseph, Mary, and Jesus."

"Well, I'm an angel and I'm the only angel who talks, so I figured I must be Hark, the herald angel."

Bud choked on his coffee.

I did get my cast off before Christmas, but I had to use crutches. It was hard for me to get anywhere in the ice and snow and I was scared of falling down and breaking it again.

I could hardly wait for Christmas Eve to arrive. Every year we had Christmas Eve with Dad's family at our house because Julie and I were the only kids and we got too many presents to haul home from anywhere else.

We always ate oyster stew for supper because it was an old family tradition. Papa brought the oysters and Great Grandma Sophie started the milk and butter cooking for the stew. Much like the ice cream Great Grandma made for the 4th of July, the oyster stew for Christmas Eve took all day to make and everyone had to take a turn at stirring the pot.

Dad took his turn during the church service. Someone had to stay and watch the stew and Dad said he and God talked all the time and they preferred to have their chats in the midst of God's glorious creation where they could hear each other better. Dad and God had a good deal going, God supplied the land and the animals and Dad took care of them and made them grow and provide for us.

Mr. Olesen had built me a tall pedestal, so I could sit high up in the air, looking down on rest of the nativity scene and the congregation. I wore a white robe and big wings made of white netting and wire, trimmed with silver Christmas tree tinsel. My halo was a circle of silver tinsel that kept sliding off my head to hang over my left eye, even though the bobby pins were supposed to keep it in place.

When all the players had assembled in their places in the manger, the spotlight shined on me and I said, "Fear not! For, behold, I bring you tidings of great joy, which shall be to all people. For unto you is born this day in the city of David a Savior, which is Christ the Lord. And this shall be a sign unto you, you shall find the babe wrapped in swaddling clothes, lying in a manger." Then I looked down at Bud, sitting in the front row where I had saved a place for him and said, "Glory to God in the highest and on Earth, peace. Peace and good will toward all men."

thirty-two

Papa started the new year of 1976 in the usual way, by taking his best girls out on the town.

Papa was a farmer with hands caked hard by dirt, who smelled of Luden's cherry cough drops, Old Spice, Brylcreme, roasted peanuts, and axle grease, but he loved a good party and boy howdy, could he dance.

Papa's life work may have called for him to wear dirty jeans and flannel shirts most of the time, but he was a snappy dresser when the occasion called for it. Each year, Papa and I went on a special shopping trip. Papa got crisp, white dress shirts he kept in a box, specially tailored slacks and jackets, and sometimes a new hat with a tiny feather on the band. I got a jewel-colored dress with a pleated skirt and black patent leather Mary Jane shoes at Christmas and a pastel-colored dress with a pleated skirt and white patent leather Mary Jane shoes at Easter. Papa was particularly fond of pleated skirts and I like to tap dance on the kitchen floor in Mary Janes, even though they left black marks that made Mom crazy mad.

On New Year's Eve, we got all slicked up in our special outfits and Papa took his girls dancing at the Elk's Club. Papa was a fabulous dancer. Great Grandma Sophie said when Papa and Aunt Toots were kids, they danced for pennies at all the barn dances and parties.

Papa and I practiced in the livingroom when we watched Lawrence Welk and sometimes when I stayed overnight, if I put on my pajamas without giving Grandma any guff, Papa would get out the dance records. We danced to all the great orchestras like Glenn Miller, Duke Ellington, and Tommy Dorsey. I liked the swing band The Mills Brothers, who did songs like _Glow Worm, It Don't Mean a Thing, Three Little Fishes,_ and _Jeepers Creepers_ and Papa liked the beat on _Cab Driver._

New's Years Eve at the Elk's Club was always special and this year was no exception. Papa bought me Shirley Temples until I was sick to my stomach. Because of my crutches, we danced like we used to when I was smaller, I took off my shoes and danced standing on top of Papa's feet.

We all watched, spellbound, as Dorothy Hamill won Olympic gold in February 1976. I, like every little girl in America, then felt I needed a Dorothy Hamill wedge cut, so I asked Grandma Cori to take me with her the next Friday I had off from school.

Friday was hair day. Grandma and many of her friends had their hair done once a week. Each week, their hair was rolled up in curlers, set under the dryer, combed out, teased into a bouffant, older lady version of a beehive, and shellacked with AquaNet hairspray, enabling the dome of hair to withstand hurricane force winds.

Hair Day was a wonder to me. I didn't like to have the snarls combed out of my baby fine hair. I did not understand why they would go to so much trouble to roll their hair in curlers, only to use a teasing comb to snarl it all up again so it was a bunch of poufy knots. I didn't like to comb my hair, but I did like to wash it so it didn't itch. Grandma and the hair ladies only had their hair washed at their weekly salon appointment. During the week, when it did get itchy, they scratched it using the rat tail end of the comb they kept around for periodic re-snarling.

Hair Day wasn't just about the hair, in fact, hair had very little to do with Hair Day. Stepping into the salon was like stepping into another world, the private domain of the hair ladies. They discussed everything and everyone in great detail and had anyone outside the confines of the salon cared to listen, to hear them tell it, the hair ladies could have provided the solution to all the problems in the universe, from what to serve at Good Cheer Club and how to get Johnny to straighten up and fly right, to how to end inflation and bring about world peace.

The rest of the winter passed much the same as the last, with everyone longing for spring and a time to start again.

Spring did arrive and Great Grandma Sophie called me over to help her plant onions. Great Grandma came out with a basket on her arm, found me a stick, and led me to the fence line.

"Poke your stick in the ground up to this notch here, then stick the bulb in the hole and pack the dirt back around it. Hairy side down, Jennie-girl, hairy side down."

I did as instructed and Great Grandma walked clear down to the other end of the fence line and started to do the same. When we finally met in the middle, I asked, "Why did we plant so many, Grandma?"

"Because a hard time is coming, Jennie-girl. I can feel it in my bones. The air doesn't hold a lick of moisture and the dust is already blowing. The rain won't be coming for a long time, just like back in the dirty 30s. We planted along the fence so it could help keep the plants from blowing away. We planted onions because their flavor makes survival edible."

thirty-three

By May, Mom's belly seemed to enter the room long before the rest of her did and such was the case one bright Saturday morning as she stood in the doorway of the livingroom with her hands braced on the door jambs.

"Jennie, I need your help."

"Not now, Mom. *Fat Albert* is on. You know I wait all week long to watch *Fat Albert*," I said without even turning my head from the TV.

"Jennie!" Mom screeched like a banshee.

My head whipped around at the shriek, "Holy smokes, Mom, what?"

"Turn off the TV. Listen. To. Me."

"Okay, okay, sheesh."

"The baby is coming right now."

"But don't you have to go to the doctor for that?"

"Listen!"

I sucked my lips inside my mouth.

"Call Grandma Cori and tell her to go out to the field and find Dad and bring him home. Then call Grandma Mae and tell her I need her. Do it now," Mom ordered, then slowly walked up the stairs, holding the walls.

I ran to the phone and started dialing.

Grandma Mae had just learned to drive and she wasn't very good at it. She came flying in the driveway and slammed on the brakes, parking sideways with half of the car up on the sidewalk and crushing the four o'clock bushes. She looked like she'd seen a ghost and her blue and white polka dotted head scarf was all kattywompus, which I soon realized was because she only had in half a head of curlers.

Dad and Grandma Cori came in next. Mom yelled from upstairs and I thought for sure Dad was going to puke in the kitchen sink.

Grandma Mae came downstairs and said, "We need help. She won't make it to the hospital. I've had babies before, but I've never been on the other side. We need someone with medical experience."

"I'll go get Bud," I said as I raced out the door.

"Bud! Bud!" I started yelling when I was still at the corner.

Bud detected the panic in my voice, dropped the tool he held in his hand, and ran to meet me in the driveway.

"Bud, you have to come quick. Mom's having the baby. She's having it right now. We need help. Grandma said we need medical help. Hurry, hurry, Bud," I begged as I tugged on his arm.

"I don't know, Jennie, I…"

"You have to do it, Bud. Mom needs you. You're the only one. C'mon!" I yelled as I started to run back to the house, dragging him behind me.

Bud washed his hands at the sink then turned to look at the stairs, but didn't move. Mom yelled again and the noise spurred Bud to action as he took the stairs two at a time.

Several minutes later, Dad came down the stairs and out the door to the truck. He came back in with a wad of baling twine in his hand and started rummaging through the silverware drawer, coming out with a steak knife.

"A steak knife, Jake?" Grandma Cori questioned.

"The man said he needed string and a knife. He's cutting meat, isn't he? What cuts meat better than a steak knife?" Dad answered.

"Cutting meat?" I thought with horror. I went out to the hay loft to wait. I didn't want to hear any more.

Virgil heard about all the excitement and came to check it out.

"What are doing up here?"

"Wondering where I'm going to sleep."

"Ah, what's wrong with sleeping in your bed?"

"I am never going near my bed again."

"Why not?"

"Because that's where Mom is having the baby."

"Why isn't she having it in her bed?"

"Because my bed has a plastic mattress cover so the mattress doesn't get wet."

"Why would it get wet?"

"Argh," I groaned in exasperation, "That's not the important part. Pay attention. I can't sleep in it again because that's where she's doing it."

"So?"

"So, do you have any idea what happens when babies are born? Have you ever seen it?"

"No."

"Well, I have. I went with Dad to check cattle a couple months ago and had to help him pull a calf. It was the most disgusting thing I've ever seen in my entire life. There was blood and slime *everywhere*. I have to assume that the same goes for baby people. Mom and the baby are up there blood and sliming my bed. Ugh."

"Wow."

Just then, everyone came out of the house carrying Mom in a sheet, put her in the backseat of the car, and Dad took off to the hospital.

"You have a new baby sister, Jennie," said Grandma Cori as she patted my back and walked back in the house.

Virgil and I walked out in the road to stand next to Bud as he stared off in the distance in the direction Mom and Dad had headed.

"That was the most amazing thing I've ever done in my life," said Bud. "Witnessing a birth instead of a death when practicing medicine shines a whole different light on things."

thirty-four

Bud had been going off on mysterious trips to the city once a week since just after Christmas. He wouldn't say what he was doing.

He went to the Memorial Day service with me this year though. The other men didn't say much, but they clapped him on the back and shook his hand.

Bud stood beside me at the cemetery services and held my hand during the trumpet playing and the gun firing. Both of us flinched at the sound of the guns, but we tightened our grips so neither of us was scared by them.

Bud knelt down to hug me and kiss my cheek when I handed him the bouquet of poppies I had saved for his friends.

"Thank you for your service, Bud," I said.

"Thank you for helping me heal my heart and find my way out of the darkness and into the sunshine, Jennie," Bud said.

Great Grandma was right, there was a hard time coming. The rain refused to fall. The wind blew and blew without relief. No matter how many times Mom vacuumed, swept, and mopped, the floors stayed gritty with dirt. We put wet towels on the floor in front of the doors to stop the dirt from blowing under them into the house. We put masking tape along the edges of the windows to stop the dirt from blowing in that way. We consolidated trips and went in and out of the house as little as possible, but still the dirt came inside. I thought it started blowing through the walls because our eggshell white walls developed wavy lines of gray dust that made the walls look like paintings of ocean waves.

The drought was so bad that a State of Emergency was declared on June 17, 1976. There seemed to be no relief in sight from the heat and the wind.

The drought wasn't the only disaster in my life. Everything was changing and I didn't like it one bit.

Papa was slowing down and Dad was doing more and more of the farm work, so Papa and Grandma were moving to town and we were moving out to their farm. I wouldn't have Virgil or Bud nearby anymore. Even though the farm was only a few miles away, I didn't want to move.

The news got worse. Virgil was moving as well. His family was moving to the next town down the road. It was only 10 miles away, but it may as well have been 10,000 since we had no way to travel that far to see each other, our parents would never let us ride our bikes that far on the highway and it would take us all day even if we could get away with it.

The final blow was that Bud would be leaving too. He had been talking with a counselor to help him with his scary thoughts and was feeling much better after coming home to rest and heal in safe and secure surroundings. He had decided to go back to medical school to finish becoming a doctor and work at the Veteran's Administration Hospital in Sioux Falls.

I was devastated.

The entire community worked to make the July 4, 1976, Bicentennial Celebration, something special.

Virgil, Julie, and I were in the parade. We were just supposed to look like pioneers in general, but I had decided we were Almonzo and Laura Ingalls Wilder with baby Rose. Aunt Toots sewed us costumes that looked just like *Little*

House on the Prairie and Uncle Henry built a miniature covered wagon for us. We tried to get Snoopy, this year's bottle calf, to pull the wagon, but he refused to cooperate, so Mr. Olesen pulled it with his antique tractor and a long rope. Uncle Henry made a plywood cutout of a horse that he attached to the rope to make it look like a horse was pulling it.

Bud, Virgil, and I sat on the edge of the ditch across the street from the park and away from the crowd to watch the fireworks display. We were all moving the following day.

"I'll be stuck here all alone," I cried. "What am I gonna do without you? I'll be the most lonesome person in the whole world."

"I won't be far away, Squirt. I'll visit sometimes, I promise. Always and forever, remember?" said Virgil.

"You'll be just fine," said Bud. "You won't be here long yourself, you know."

"Where am I going?"

"Off to see the world," replied Bud.

"I'll never get out of here," I complained.

"Yes, you will," said Bud. "You will follow your dreams and go on grand adventures. And you'll take Virgil and me and all of your other friends and family with you, for you forever carry pieces of each of us in your heart. If the great, wide world beyond the prairie hurts you or makes you weary, you can always come home to heal and rest because when you need it, those pieces of us all will build the road home.

the end

...or maybe just a new beginning

20546558R00131

Made in the USA
Middletown, DE
30 May 2015